T0193527

GM & GS PRIVATE INVESTIGATION SERVICE

BOOK V

D. H. CROSBY

authorHOUSE®

AuthorHouse™
1663 Liberty Drive
Bloomington, IN 47403
www.authorhouse.com
Phone: 1 (800) 839-8640

Published by AuthorHouse   06/23/2018

ISBN: 978-1-5462-4832-3 (sc)
ISBN: 978-1-5462-4831-6 (e)

Print information available on the last page.

PART NINETEEN

CHAPTER ONE

Four years later....

Unitus was in juvenile courtroom defending his client Jerry C. Anderson. He was accused of stealing a bicycle from another teenager.

"Henry, may I call you Henry?" Unitus said walking up to face the chair where Henry sat. Henry's eyes were increasing in size as this huge man stood in front of him.

"Yes, it's okay," his voice quivering.

"Is it true, you stole Jerry C. Anderson 's cell phone? Just answer yes or no," Unitus instructed him.

"And my client was simply borrowing your bicycle because he had no phone to call his girlfriend and had to ride over to her house?" Unitus stood still looking at Henry.

"MY father said I had to," Henry said.

"Answer the question yes or no," Unitus stated.

"I object your honor. He is leading..." the other lawyer said.

"Overruled. Answer the question," the judge said.

"Yes, sir! I broke the phone and my father said, I had to get my bike back." Henry never raised his head for his father would be furious with him.

"The phone value would exceed the price of the old bicycle, would it not? And your father would be madder, if he had to replace that expensive phone. Would he not?" Unitus asked.

"Objection leading again, your honor," the lawyer insisted.

"Overruled. Answer the question," the judge said.

"Yes, sir," Henry admitted.

"So if we dismissed this case, you would accept Jerry having your bicycle as a replacement for his phone?" Unitus suggested.

Henry's father nodded.

"Yes, sir. That would be great!" he said.

"Let me confer with my client," Unitus walked to the table.

Jerry agreed because his mother had already got him a new phone. He nodded his head and smiled.

"Okay," the judge said, "and young man," looking at Henry. "I do not want to see you in my court on stealing charges in the future. Let this be a lesson. The case is closed and the court is adjourned."

The gavel was whacked, and the judge left the courtroom since it was the last case on the docket.

Adriana had sat in the back of the court, watching her handsome husband do a superb job and was grinning. He had that cobalt blue business suit on that she loved. His cobalt eyes were searching the courtroom for her.

There she was in that gray striped suit that he loved. With her sandy colored hair piled on her head and held with a single white clasp. He sighed, "She's mine."

Standing in those three inch white high heels with ankle straps that he loved. It was mere torture just to watch her walk. She swayed those hips coming toward him, and stood in front of him smiling, as she watched him drool.

At least once a year, they recreated their first meeting in the courthouse. She was still toned and svelte, and he was still ripped from training for his yearly triathlon with the vets.

This was the day that took their breaths away. As they spoke to each other, neither could look away.

She finally said, "Want to get that big .... briefcase and take me ……... to lunch?"

"I had better do just that before I embarrass both of us," he walked to the desk and retrieved the briefcase, and escorted her to the van.

He lifted her inside, and her skirt rode up which exposed her no undies condition, that only he could see. "It is a shame I have to say close those gorgeous legs and close them now. We are in the middle of town … or else!" he whispered.

Adriana teased, "Or else what?"

He was stammering, "Or else I will take you right here!"

"Here, there and everywhere. Remember?" she asked seductively.

Unitus came closer and she closed her legs, and put the door in between them. "It is daytime!" she giggled. "You really would!"

"You are right. It was dark that night, the moon shining!"

He shook his head. The kids were both in preschool, Angel was five and Vanderbilt was four, and this was ten thirty in the morning.

Unitus asked, "Where would you like to go to lunch?" and he grinned from ear to ear knowing her answer.

Adriana wet her lips and did not look at him, but raised her skirt to her hips, turned and unbuttoned her blouse, "Guess?"

"Stop or I will not be able to drive. It is growing and if it stops the steering wheel, we may hit something before I get you home," he stated as a fact.

"Fair enough can't have my plaything hurt in any way, shape, form, or fashion! I need it too badly," she purred.

"Don't talk Adriana! That has an affect on … geez look what you have done to my suit?" he said and grinned.

"Complaining counselor?" she rolled her eyes at him.

"No Darling, but we are not making it home!" he told her.

"I know. Ain't love grand?" and they pulled off at the same place, they did the first time. Off the interstate, and made passionate love in the back of the van.

They saw the blue light and the officer got out. Unitus got in the front seat and Adriana stayed in the back.

"Hey, Mr. Universe! Just checking to see if you were having car trouble. Everything okay?" It was the same officer that Adriana had broke his hand the night that Angel was born.

"No, just got a little sleepy. Stopped to regroup. All is good.

Had to splash water in my face," explaining why his face was so wet. He was really perspiring with the workout that he and Adriana had just had. She was grinning and being very still.

4

"Well... I am glad everything is okay. Tell that strong wife of yours, hello for me," and he flexed his hand and walked back to his patrol car.

"My darling, we have to leave the highway before we get a ticket. Do you agree?" he asked furrowing his eyebrows. "And put some clothes on before someone sees my prize!"

"Oh, I think on the top of a mountain no one will see me, but you!" and she sat there pouting.

"Don't make me come back there, Adriana!" he grinned into the rear-view mirror.

She stretched her legs to the roof of the van.

"I am warning you, Adriana. I may run off the road," Unitus was panting.

"You would not dare. We have three more hours, if you hurry!" she pointed out.

He stepped on the gas. She popped him on the back of the head. "Don't get a ticket. I will have to defend you in a court of law, and I want to be doing other things!" she said reaching around for him.

"Don't do that Adriana, please I am dying here! Look if you don't believe me!" she was grinning and they were on the road with the long white fence. He stopped since it was private property and climbed into the back.

"I've had enough torture, now you must pay the price!" he shouted.

"Bring it on big boy! Oh yes, Unitus! I ..." he had his mouth on hers, and she was unable to say another word.

An hour later, he climbed into the front seat leaving her curled in a ball of bliss in the back.

"That will keep you quiet until we get home!" he was proud of himself.

"Yes, Unitus. We are almost to the bottom of the mountain so I guess I can wait maybe or maybe not. Just joking! You did superb, honey. That's the problem." He was speeding again and up the mountain, they went.

"We have one and one half hours before the kids get home. Get in my arms and I will take you to our bed," he said. She jumped out of the van and into his arms.

"Just like old times. We still can't get enough of a good thing. You are so good and I think it gets better and better," Adriana said.

"If it got any better, I'd be dead," Unitus said as he nuzzled her breast and made his way to her navel.

"You got to stop!" she said.

"Stop?" he questioned.

"Taking your time. We are home! I want it fast and furious," and she giggled as he did just that.

"You know … I may never walk again Unitus!" she was squeezing her legs around his waist.

He said, "Good! Stay in bed all day and night. Fine with me. Walking is overrated. Seriously I have done my triathlon for today and tomorrow. The KIDS?" they both jumped up!

"Mercy that was close!" Unitus said.

Looking at his wife cooking supper as he sat in the recliner pretending to read the newspaper.

The kids came running in, followed by Kyleigh and Madison. They took turns picking up the kids. Kyleigh 's day was today and Adriana's was tomorrow.

They all jumped on Unitus. They all still thought he was the monkey bars. He would let them climb up his massive body and hang there. Sometimes two on one arm and one on the other.

He got a break today because the seven of Roscoe's had other activities this afternoon. He probably would not survive all of them today, but tomorrow no problem. He loved to play with them all.

They called him Mr. Universe like the rest of the people in the community which didn't bother him as long as Adriana didn't call him that. When she called him that, she was mad and he did not want to see her angry.

She was hard to handle without that added to the mix.

His wife was a fire cracker and he loved that about her. She would fight to the bitter end … if she thought she was right. So he usually would say, "Yes dear." It saved a lot of confrontation.

But if he wanted some great makeup sex, he would spar with her verbally and grin. Then when he ceded that made her even madder! Oh my goodness! Just the thought conjured up a delightful time, they had last month.

She stopped to talk to Kyleigh and wiped her hands on her apron over her skinny jeans.

Kyleigh said, "I see you got some, too!"

Adriana frowned, how did Kyleigh know she had got SOME. Was it written across her forehead, she might as well admit it. "Yeah!"

Kyleigh said, "Don't you just love the way they wear?"

She looked down and she had the same kind of skinny jeans that Kyleigh had on, "Yeah just love them, they are so comfortable!" smiling at Unitus who was looking up at her and gave a wink.

"They have the same effect on my Guy! Speaking of … I got to do the same thing!" she said.

Adriana said, "COOK?" and Kyleigh was to the door.

"Yes, cook. Tomorrow is my day for you to pick them up," and she winked at Adriana and walked out.

Unitus saw it and walked over to Adriana as the door was closed, "and we know what they will be doing tomorrow, don't we Darling!"

"Yes Dear! We women have our codes just like you men. So don't spread the word, or else!" Adriana continued cooking.

He was behind her and grabbed her pulling her back on him.

"Don't start something we cannot finish," she said.

"That is so true. It wouldn't take long? You have me begging for more already. Geez! I am a whipped man!" he grinned at her.

"And don't you forget it!" she smiled and batted her eyelashes at him as he went off to play with the kids.

CHAPTER TWO

Beatrice and Roscoe's first set of twins, Cain and Caleb were now seven and in first grade. The second set of twins, BeBe and FiFi were six and in kindergarten. The triplets Jill, Jessie and Johnny were five and now in Pre-K. The house was empty all day.

Roscoe said, "Beatrice that vasectomy was the best thing we have ever done for each other. Don't you agree my green-eyed beauty?" as he reached under the covers in the middle of the afternoon.

"Oh, my Darling! I'd say having you swing by every day at one time or the other for a nooner is absolutely the best solution to our dilemma." and she nuzzled his ear and pushed him to the door. They had the kids in all sorts of activities after school and nonstop until bedtime, bath time and homework time. Then they were exhausted parents of SEVEN kiddos.

"You have to go to work to feed the children. Go! I'll see you tomorrow!" knowing all the time that he would be home at five thirty on the dot, and she waved and blew him a kiss.

Kyleigh on the other hand was not rushing to have another child. Madison was seven and had plenty of children to play with. All his cousins lived across the street, plus Unitus and Adriana's two kids at the top of the mountain.

"Why would I want more?" she answered when Guy asked.

"No, I really I don't. But if you want more, we will try!"

Madeline and Trevor were as spry as ever and truly enjoying the boathouse and lazy days on the lake. He fished and she read her books. The small yacht was an oasis for them to get away from the family and hide out. Yet close enough, if someone needed them.

Michelle and Robert were four years into their marriage and traveling to all the major cities in the USA and abroad for his lectures. He never left home without her by his side.

She had got so use to being Michelle that she rarely thought of her former self "Raven." For awhile she had the fear that someone would recognize her, and would kill her and Robert.

"You are being ridiculous," she told herself. She had nothing that looked like Raven only a small tat on her left butt cheek remained. It was a four leaf clover for good luck. She had the rest of her tattoos laser removed, and she never let this one show to the public.

On one trip to Hawaii she had worn a sexy swimsuit for Robert and her clover showed. "You can't let all my colleagues see that beautiful tattoo, they may want to kiss it like I do," and he laughed. She never wore it again.

If it was one of Jung's men, he would stun her and feed her to alligators. She had witnessed another tattooed girl come to that fate. She braced herself and clung to the balcony rail.

"Are you okay, Darling?" he placed a hand on the small of her back and drew her to him.

"I am fine. Just homesick," she felt safe there. Nowhere else, but she would not let Robert know because he loved his work. She wanted him to be happy in everything.

Michellee smiled up at Robert, and he said, "We will go home tomorrow, and I can reschedule the other two lectures for later in the year."

"Thank you, I really need to see my family. I miss them!" then she saw a man in a black suit walking toward them. He looked familiar, and as he got closer.

She knew him to be a HIT MAN, and he was going to kill Robert first so she could watch, and then her. She quickly twirled around Robert and karate kicked him, up beside the head and took his gun. Handing it to Robert to hold as he stood with his mouth open. She took the man's hand and stretched his arm out, and put her foot on his neck and with one small jerk, dislocated his shoulder, "That should hold him."

"Close your mouth, Dear! Put the gun in your pocket in case we need it." He did and she smiled at him.

They walked hand in hand back to their room chatting per usual. Inside their room, she was methodically cleaning the weapon of all fingerprints, and putting it in the Kleenex box.

"You had better fess up Lassie because I am unnerved, but also impressed that my sweet little wife can protect herself and her dumb husband at the same time. Don't we agree, he is a dumb bloke?" Robert was fascinated, but angry with her.

He was staring at her and she at him. "We have got to move or you will not have a wife. They will kill me, like they did Haruto!" She was shoving clothes in the suitcases and he knew, if she did NOT fold their clothes precisely that it was serious!

He began calling for the last flight out tonight for their destination was the Charlotte airport. They left Hawaii and landed in Los Angeles, then departed after a one hour layover. From LAX, they continued on to North Carolina on the same airplane.

He was going to ask, and she kissed him, "We will talk when we get home … not until then … please understand."

She smiled and touched his face saying, "I love you so much!" She closed her eyes and finally slept as he watched for whomever may want to harm her.

Robert was thinking and could not wrap his head around the magnitude of expertise his beautiful wife had in the martial arts. He had never seen anyone take an armed man down like she had. Haruto … this man must have taught her extensively how to defend herself. She had said he save not only her life, but the entire Porter family.

Trevor could give him the answers he needed, if Michelle shut down on him. He needed to be informed, if someone was trying to kill his wife. He would protect her at any cost.

She was so peaceful when she was asleep.

She was a handful in the bedroom, and a really creative designer in her business. She did not want him to travel without her. Was she trying to protect him, or was she so in love with him that she wanted him day and night as he wanted her?

They touched down at midnight and James was there with the white limo to get them. When they arrived home, they went straight to their bedroom, and he was going to question her, but she was having none of it. She had him panting before he could remove his clothes.

Yes, she was an expert at making love to him. She knew all his pleasure zones in four years. She had mastered them all. He had in return learned all of her erotic fantastic positioning that intensified any coupling. They may engage in them any given night. Never was one time enough, "gotta to make you miss me when you're not here with me," she would say.

Miss was not in his vocabulary when it came to her. He longed for her touch every minute of every day. The only time that that vanished was when he stepped into her arms, and he gave her free reign. The longing was at that time slaked. Then the vicious cycle started all over again as automatic as breathing.

They lay naked and in a peaceful dream state and he said, "You promised to talk to me and now is the time. You have waited four years and now time is up. You must tell me everything."

"Do you think you can handle the truth?" she stared at the ceiling while he stared at her.

"I am Raven, one of Mao Jung's hit men. You know the notorious Drug Lord of Japan. Haruto and I brought him down. He is in prison. I was hired to kill the Porters, but Haruto worked for them. He fell in love with me and changed my thoughts to good, and hopeful thoughts for the first time in my life. The day we brought Jung down, Haruto took a bullet for me and died a martyr. The Porters were safe after Jung was in prison," she wiped a tear from her cheek.

"They loved Haruto. They did not want his death to be for nothing, nor did I. So they got me in a safe house and gave me a new name, schooling, clothing, an apartment, but most of all they loved me enough to adopted me. I love them dearly. Now you know it all. That man recognized me. How I don't know, but there will always be someone out there wanting to kill me. So you can run away from me, and I will understand. I prefer you to go ... and not stay and be a target. I love you that much. Go!" and she buried her head in the pillow and sobbed.

He grabbed her and folded her body into his arms, "I will never leave you Michelle. My Michelle! Don't cry, it tears me up to see you cry. I married you forever till death do us part! We can face anything together. Do you want to talk to Trevor or do you want me to? He must know about this as soon as possible. He may already know."

She had turned her head away and began to rise, standing by the window to stare at the stars. "When I was little, I ask the man in the moon to help me. He never could. It would be best, if I left the Porters and you. No one would bother you 'all. If I vanished, they would not come here."

She had made up her mind. He could see it in her eyes.

"Don't you dare leave me! Don't you dare think it EVER!"

He grabbed her, "You want to kill me. Leave and it will kill me. It would not take a bullet to kill me. Do you hear what I am saying? Answer me, Michelle?" Robert was kissing her and holding her and for the first time ... she was not responding. Just a blank stare on her face, one that he had never seen before.

He dare not leave this room. He held her hand and dialed with his other hand. "Trevor can you and Madeline come to our room now. It is real important," and he hung up without waiting for an answer. He held her lifeless body in his arms after getting her into her long robe.

They knocked, and saw what state she was in. Madeline held her and rocked her while Robert filled Trevor in on what happened in Hawaii.

He saw the terror in Robert's eyes when he said she would leave so we would be safe. "Trevor she meant it! Help me! She cannot walk away from her family to save us! We must make her know that we will fight for her." Robert was not an emotional man, but this was making him come unglued.

"Calm down. Everything is going to work out. We as a family will convince her. I'll call the troops in! You stay with her and if you can't, tell Madeline and she will stay with her," Trevor made that clear.

"Thank you, sir! Thank you, I will!" Robert went to hold Michelle and took over for Madeline to go with Trevor.

"The man, if he took pictures. They know her new identity. Robert is right they will be here. We must be ready!"

Guy had just got to GM & GS Private Investigation Service opening the mail and drinking a cup of coffee when he got a call from Trevor. He filled him in on the situation.

"Michelle is not doing well. Can you call Kyleigh 's doctor and have him go by the house and see her?" Trevor asked. "Will do and I'll work on getting this man's name in

15

Hawaii and I'll round up our team. Roscoe can put extra security there."

"Tell Robert we are here for him, too," Guy said.

"He needs to hear that from you," Trevor said.

"That is true. I'll give Roscoe a call and Unitus can tell Marcus."

Marcus Buchanan was furious that someone would want to harm that pretty little Michelle, and he added men to guard the Porters. He told Eunice so she could let Jason, Corey, and Adam know what was going on and for them to steer clear of any visits right now.

Janice was walking really well now and Adam was smiling.

"My wife, four years ago could barely walk and look at her running around the house good as new," Adam was so proud of her recovery, but refused to let her go back to work in security."You can do that office work. I put my foot down."

Janice loved him being in charge of everything. Just the way he made her feel so special, during her car wreck and recovery. She cherished those days. It made their marriage stronger.

They still had not spoke of the death of their baby and she never would. It was Justin's baby, and that would have been a lie to live with. That lie could have torn, them apart. Justin's death had made her do some stupid things, but the decision to walk into Adam's room that night was the best thing that could ever happen to her.

If they had a child in the future, it would be Adam's and only Adam's. That was a topic she had changed her mind and was ready now to discuss it with him. That night she did.

"Do you want a baby Adam?" Janice asked as they lay in the bed staring at each other. They liked to do that every night just stare, and rub, and play with each other. It validated that their life was real, not just a fairy tale in their heads.

"All that you want, I want. If you want a baby, then I want a baby! I am surely going to have fun trying to make a baby. If you say you do, we can start tonight!" he said grinning.

Now that he was on a first shift maintenance crew schedule. They had a normal schedule and that is what a child needed. Parents to be at home with them at night.

Janice said, "I am off the pill from this night on. If it happens, it happens." They told her after breaking her pelvis, she may have trouble conceiving. She wrapped her arms around his neck, and he drew her naked body over him. He was still not going to put any pressure on her.

"You tell me what and how you want it, Baby?" and she did want him to go slow and easy at first. Then she said,"Turn me over and do me good like you did the first night. It will make me feel so good about my recovery! Don't keep holding back, afraid I will break. If it hurts, I will let you know. OK?"

It did not hurt. "Oh my goodness! Adam! Adam!" and she was moving like they had not done in a long long time, and it was so good that Adam was reeling back and forth waiting for her. All of a sudden she started vibrating, and making those sounds that he loved to hear and she was over the moon.

She had raised to the top and back down, and up and back down, and then he had to let it go for the first time. He was pounding her good, and she was loving it!

At the end, Janice held him and said, "Honey we just made a baby! There is no doubt in my mind. That was the BEST! If we didn't you are going to have to try it over and over again, just like that!"

Adam was lying there beside her quietly getting his breath back, "I'm going to have to do this every night until. You are, right? Damn straight! I am going to be a happy man either way. My wife makes me so happy," he grinned at her.

"Can we do it again just to make sure we did it good enough," Adam laughed.

Janice stretched leaning on one elbow, and nodded her head up and down. "Bring it on!"

CHAPTER THREE

Tate came in the office and said, "Morning Boss!" He slung his portable office satchel over on the desk.

"Did you talk to Trevor this morning?" Tate asked.

Guy nodded his head, and Tate said, "Ain't that something? Just when you thought the coast was clear!"

"GM is watching Michelle close. I heard Trevor tell her, if they didn't watch her that she was going to run, and she would be a dead duck!" Tate and Guy would be helping to see that didn't happen.

"Yeah! She's the kind of person that would sacrifice herself for the family. Geez! Bet Robert is going crazy!" Guy thought out loud.

"You know it!" Tate said thinking of Debbie. "I know I would be!"

"That reminded me to call for the doctor to check on her." He got Kyleigh 's doctor on the phone, and he agreed to go out and check on Michelle this morning.

Guy gave him a head's up, "Doctor, they say she is just sitting and staring. That's all I know. Thank you, just send me the bill!" Guy hung up and walked to the window. "We cannot do anything until Trevor calls, so we must sit tight!"

Guy was having flashbacks of when Kyleigh was abducted, and a shiver went down his spine. The vision of that filthy Jared Banks brutalizing his wife was still embedded in his psyche. Even though the man was dead, it still haunted him that he was not there to protect her.

"I pray the fiends don't take Michelle. If she leaves this homestead, they may well get the chance. Robert has no clue whom we are dealing with, but I know Tate," he gritted his teeth and turned to get a commitment from Tate.

"I'm in Guy. This is one of my family members, too. Even though we are not blood kin, I love all of you. I will fight against anyone that wants to do any of us harm," Tate continued to organize the cases that he had been working on.

Guy called Kyleigh, "I just called to say I love you that's all, and that we have a busy day planned here. I will give you a call, if I will be late, bye." She must not know about Michelle unless absolutely necessary.

It was their day that Kyleigh did not have to pick up the kids, and usually they made love all day. He was so looking forward to it, and he knew she was also. By calling early about his work, she would not think anything was amiss. She would save his surprise for tonight! Dang, I can't wait to get home. He had turned away from Tate.

Tate grinned because since Debbie had been working so hard at the Casino, she had been coming home so tired. This day was her day off, and he was going to take a tip from Guy and give his wife a call. "I just called to say I love you that's all, and that we have a busy day planned here. I will call, if I will be late, bye."

Guy had turned his chair around and was looking at Tate, "Copycat!" furrowing his brow as if he was perturbed.

Tate said, "I'm learning from a master!"

"Well ... in that case ... it's alright!" and Guy grinned.

Debbie overheard Trevor on the phone calling the FBI and notifying them that they needed to get Michelle to another safe house that one of Jung's men had appeared, and tried to harm her in Hawaii.

That could be why Tate called her? He wanted her to stay at home today, and wait for him. She would not leave for any reason. The fear had numbed her body that same fear that she had squashed, so long ago. Poor Michelle. She would be there for her, if she wanted to talk. Madeline must be in the room with her.

Robert was pacing outside of Trevor's office. He also heard what Trevor said. He said to himself that the FBI could not take her from him. He would not let them, "Trevor !" He walked into the den. "They can't take her away from me!"

"Sit down, Son. Do you want her to be safe? We may can work something out. Just be patient. Now go and spend as much time with her as you can." Trevor encouraged him.

"You are right! I am so tired. I slept none last night. I was afraid to go to sleep!" Robert said.

"Okay sit there, and take a nap in my recliner. I will watch for you! A man needs to be ALERT and sleep deprivation is a bummer," he pointed to the chair and went back to his computer data and printouts.

Robert slept for two hours and then he went to check on his wife. Madeline and she were still chatting, and Michelle was sharing design sketches. She was actually giggling with glee as she talk to GM.

He waltzed in and smiled, "My two favorite ladies seem to be deep in Michelle's workbook. Aren't they fantastic? Isn't she the most artistic at everything she does?"

"Yes and yes. We are two of your biggest fans, my dear. I must go check on Trevor, and find Debbie so we can start a fabulous supper." She kissed Michelle and went out the door.

"I thought you were never coming back," Michelle was teary eyed. He took her in his arms and quenched his thirst. She climbed his body and put her legs around his waist and he walked with her attached to the door and locked it.

She was not going to let him go for any reason.

"Honey stand for a moment," and she did, but would not let go of his neck. She was staring at him, he was having a time.

"You are amazing!" she kissed him and pulled his coat off.

"I am obsessed with my own wife, but you know that!"

"I want you to miss me when I am gone. You know I have to leave one way or the other," she was being truthful.

"Don't talk like that. Wherever you go, I will be with you!

You cannot leave without me. We are attached," he emphasizing that he had not released her.

They made love till the doctor knocked on the door.

Robert kissed her, "We don't need the doctor anymore. My wife is back to normal!" He shouted and grinned at her.

"I need only you to make me well," Michelle said.

"Madeline make him go away please!" she said kissing Robert and loving him again until night came. She knew she was leaving and would not be back. He would have to sleep, and then she would exit. That was her plan. He usually got sleepy afterward, but not this time.

She must be doing something wrong. His stamina only increased, and she was loving it. It was just, she was getting sleepy instead of him.

That nap he took not only gave him much needed sleep, but the best reward ever. This was a learning experience for him to have a marathon with his wife, he must nap beforehand.

"You are the master tonight! I forfeit my title," and she slept.

He sat in the chair and watched her breathe, even in an unconscious state, she was beautiful. He dare not move or he would be reminded of his need for her! He dare not sleep.

Madeline asked, "Trev have you notified the guards around the house and asked them to bring her back, if she tries to run. She will you know."

"I know, and yes I have. She loves all of us so much, she will do anything to draw the danger away from us. Poor Robert has no idea what she went through. I just think he is in denial about the severity of the situation. He's a smart man academically but..." Trevor said.

"But what Trevor? You think I was raised in the upper crust and don't know what goes on in the ghetto. Don't you?"

"Where is Michelle?" Trevor evaded Robert's question.

"Debbie is in with her, and promised not to leave until I returned. Answer me?"

"Madeline go in with the girls, please!" Trevor wanted her out of Robert's firing line.

"Of course, dear. Just holler if you need me," she left the two men squaring off. That was a joke!

"Have a seat, Robert!" Trevor pointed to a chair near him.

"I prefer to stand," he knew if he sat, he may fall asleep like last time. He had been awake all night.

"You haven't slept any as I would, if it were Madeline. We men think we are indivisible and nothing is too large that we cannot handle it by ourselves. Well there are things I cannot protect Madeline from. I have to ask for help. I'm enough of a man to know when I need help. Are you?" Trevor stared at him.

"I know and I thank you. I am tired and not thinking clearly.

I thank you for everything you are doing? She loves you all so much. She will run I know it, and it terrifies me?" he broke down and held his head in his hands and tears flowed. "I don't think I can live without her."

Trevor rose and stood by him and patted him on the back. "I know, Son. We will watch her. You get some sleep. You have NIGHT duty."

Robert went to the recliner and slept because he trusted Trevor. He had made a fool of himself.

The agent came in the room and talked to Trevor, "We can get her another safe house and a new identity, but he is so well known that it will be hard to hide him," looking at Robert.

"She will not go without him. I know my Michelle. You can disguise him with hair dye and beard. Come on! We have to save these kids. She gave so much to capture that fiend Jung?" Trevor was a good negotiator. Robert was listening, but did not move or open his eyes.

"OK. OK. You win Trevor. I'll see what I can do," and they shook hands and the agent left.

"Robert go to sleep!" Trevor said.

Robert smiled and did not speak, but went into a sound sleep this time.

He would tell Michelle tonight so it would ease her mind that they would be together. There was no doubt in Robert's mind.

She was relieved and promised, "I will NOT run, if you are going with me! I can see the safe house differently."

CHAPTER FOUR

Marcus and Eunice were going to see the new grandson Mark Vanderbilt Pommel and the little Angel. Eunice had knitted him a blue blanket with expensive lame thread.

"It is beautiful and Adriana will love it. She loves her kids to have nice things that her daddy brings, and this is nice Eunice. It is very special because you made it which makes it priceless," and he kissed her.

Marcus did not care who saw him kiss his wife. In years gone by, he displayed no affection in public. When Unitus opened the door, he was still kissing Eunice.

She blushed and Unitus smiled, and patted his father-in-law on the back as Eunice came around the corner with the present.

"Way to go! Come on in the house, Marcus. The kids are in their rooms and neither are asleep! So what do you say, you help me tire them out! That way they will sleep tonight!" and Unitus laughed.

"Sounds good to me! I want to see little Mark and my little Angel. I've been trying all day to get away from THE CASINO and get here to have some granddaddy fun."

He kissed Adriana on the head, and the men headed for the boy's room where Vanderbilt was playing with his trucks, and Angel came running out of her room.

"Granddaddy Granddaddy!" Angel shouted and jumped in his outstretched arms. Unitus gathered up Vanderbilt. No way was he calling his son Mark. Marcus could, though.

The women were chatting away, and Adriana was telling her how beautiful the blanket was. Adriana asked if she would teach her to knit.

Adriana could no more sit still long enough to learn to knit anything, but she wanted Eunice to feel special and she agreed.

Her daddy had done good this time. She liked Eunice from the first Christmas party at the Porters. They had always been able to talk with ease.

"How are Jason, Corey and Adam doing? I hear from Janice and Ellen because they stop by, and play with the kids every now and then," Adriana said.

"Jason is doing better now. He is back in school. Corey is working and taking night classes. Ellen has been keeping Janice company in the day, and helped her recover from that automobile accident. Her recovery has been remarkable. She still refuses to drive," Eunice reported.

"You have a house full," Adriana laughed.

"It is not full by any means and we want you and Unitus to bring the kids by anytime. Truly we must plan a play date once a week!" Eunice invited them.

"Yes I have finally admitted it was harder to recover from the C-section. Now he is pre-K, I am doing FINE," and she winked at Unitus, and he turned the other way.

"Dang!" the baby's blanket was in the other room and he went to get it. Adriana was driving him up the wall now. She said that knowing it would turn him on.

He still remembered those six weeks without sex. That was sheer torture. Even now when he thought about it after all these years. They were back to full steam ahead. She smiled as he returned. Little Vanderbilt loved for his daddy to rock him, but tonight he let Marcus rock him.

Eunice was smiling at Adriana and pointing to Marcus. "He is really enjoying that after the stressful day he has had!"

"What do you mean?" Adriana asked.

"He had to fire the Chef at THE CASINO and met with the staff. It seems the Chef was drinking on the job and cursing at the staff. Poor Debbie never said a word, but the others reported him. When Marcus found out how Debbie had been talk to … that Henri was out the door! I was so proud of your father," and she smiled at him.

"I gave Debbie the job and she is now my Master Chef! I told her that she can redo the menu anyway she likes. I hope it will be Southern Cooking, but it is entirely up to her," and Marcus continued rocking his namesake.

Unitus said, "Yum yum We may have to go to the casino for supper from now on Honey!"

Adriana rolled her eyes at him, "Are you saying I don't cook well?"

"Adriana Honey, you don't cook at all!" Unitus held his head to the side staring at her.

"That's a good point, Dear. You are right!" and they all laughed.

"I'm going to learn one day and won't have all this free time to play with …." Unitus interrupted her.

"With the children! With the children!" their agreement was he would cook and she would play with him extra for not doing that chore! He definitely did not want her cooking, if it messed up their playtime after the kids were asleep.

He was grinning at her and she blew him an air kiss which hit him below the belt.

He closed his eyes and grabbed the new blue lame blanket complimenting on how pretty it was and how soft it was.

Adriana knew... IT wasn't soft anymore, and she grinned.

Unitus gave her a 'I will get you for this later' look, and agreed with whatever her daddy was saying.

When they walked them to the door, Eunice said, "We have enjoyed this so much. Call me anytime Adriana, and we will have you' all over for supper one night soon."

"Do come daughter? Eunice cooks the best southern foods. Maybe she can teach you," Marcus suggested.

"You do mean Unitus Daddy, don't you?" staring at Unitus.

"Miss Eunice, I would LOVE to learn how to cook southern fried chicken," Unitus grinned at Adriana. Then she kissed him on the cheek, and rested on his hip.

"Okay! If you 'all come early, I will teach you both." Eunice was so happy to have something she could do for the family, and Marcus was beaming.

"That's a dinner date! We will talk soon."

They left after kissing on the kids and putting them to bed.

Unitus grabbed Adriana and kissed her saying, "You will not be cooking any fried chicken, but mine!"

She nodded, "Whatever you say, Darling!"

Debbie was telling Tate what had happened, and the stress she was now under. He held her because she was shaking so badly, and walked her to their room. "Are you sure you want to take on that big of a responsibility?"

She looked so fragile, but she loved her job.

"I have always wanted to have a job like this. It is a once in a lifetime job. I want to do well. Mr. Marcus has been so good to me. I don't want to let him down. I don't want to let myself down," Debbie said.

"That settles it Master Chef! You may need a stress reliever. Do you?" Tate kissed her neck and she was undoing his shirt.

"I think that is exactly what I need," she had no time to spare before he picked her up, and marched with her in his arms to the shower.

Later she said, "This chef is so glad her husband knows how to cook in the bedroom because that was the best dish I have tasted all day, and it was served to perfection!"

Beatrice was not looking out the window for nothing. It was Roscoe's birthday, and he was not on time. She stood there in a fancy dress that Kyleigh had helped her pick out.

The kids would be home from school any minute. So she took the dress off and pulled on her skinny jeans, and a denim top. She sent him a text: TOO LATE MISTER … LOL

He had been too busy to call. It was a lame excuse, but truthful. The seven handfuls were coming in the door now.

All the noise came inside with them. She smiled and had each one hang up their coat on their very own coat peg. Their very own peg with their name over it.

The little triplets did everything the bigger kids did. That was great until they get older, and she laughed at the thought of them all having their own driver's license. OMG! I think I will jog Roscoe's brain.

"Honey, we are having the time of our lives with these Tonka trucks, so don't miss out! Come on home baby, just think in a few years they will be driving cars!" she grinned. She could feel the shiver that went up his spine at the thought, and he was fifteen miles away at the security office.

"I am sorry about not calling, I have been swamped. I have to tell you something … but you cannot tell Kyleigh. Do you promise?"

"Of course, I do! Shoot!" and he filled her in on Michelle. She immediately went to the front window and looked out but unable to see Madeline and Trevor's house from there. It was around the bend. She saw Kyleigh in her yard with Madison.

"Roscoe! Guy has to tell her. She and Madison are in the front yard playing. They would be easy targets, if not for the security, and that big black dog. She reached down and rubbed her Dynamite 's head. I am going to call her and ask her to come here until you two get home. Okay?"

"OK … I see your point. We'll see you tonight. Love you!" and he hung up and walked out of his office, and up to his secretary 's desk.

"Freda, I'm going to GM & GS Private Investigation Service. Dang I still get a thrill out of saying that! If you need me TEXT me. Those jokers have teased me enough. They say I'm old fashioned," Roscoe laughed.

"Don't look at me when you say OLD or I'll fashion a new lunch special … mud in the face. That's what the spa treatment has to make you look young these days," and she winked.

"You would not tell my wife that would you?" Roscoe was thinking of Beatrice in a mud wrestling outfit and slithering around. "OMG!" he turned to Freda and said, "I think that's a great idea." She about fell out of her chair.

He was mumbling to himself on the way to his Silverado. "Text is Tate 's middle name," Roscoe laughed. He always suggested it in the library. He had to text Debbie instead of calling her.

"Now he wants me to learn how," Roscoe still mumbling.

"So I can be more hip," air quotation marks. Inscoe had been watching him and he fell into step as they walked.

"You okay, Boss?" Inscoe knew he was not himself today.

"Another family member crisis. There's something NEW. They gotta put Michelle in a safe house again," with a nod.

"Oh man, I thought that was over?" Inscoe said.

"Me, too! Me, too! See you later. Hold down the fort," Roscoe requested.

"Will do! Will do!" Sgt. Inscoe turned back around and walked toward the security building shaking his head.

Roscoe was going to touch base with Trevor after he talked to Guy, and got him to come home with him. Tate agreed to stick close to home and make sure Debbie stayed safe. Being that they lived with Trevor and Madeline, they were secure.

Adam had no knowledge of what was happening until Tate came by to see him at the hotel. He walked with him and they talked.

"Make sure Marcus and Eunice know. So Jason, Corey and Ellen stay put. You and Janice doing okay?"

"Yeah, she is amazing. She wants to come back to work, but I don't want her to be in security work like she was before. Trying to get her to just work in the office. We'll see. Thanks Bro, for the heads up," Adam said.

Tate parked in the back of the casino where Debbie worked, and sat watching her as he got a cup of coffee.

She was hustling around the kitchen and asking people to do this and that, and really making the supper display a masterful buffet.

She waved at him and strutted to his table, "May I help you sir?" Debbie said smiling.

"I'd like a slice of ... are you ready to go pie?"

"Yes I am. Let me get my coat. Meet you out back," she flew through the aisle and an arm grabbed her.

The man was a burly lumberjack and she called for security and she said, "Don't you EVER come near me again or you will be dead, Mister!"

"Sorry must be the liquor that is free here. It went to my head. I do apologize, ma'am!" looking at the guards.

Kirk Matterhorn was not use to females talking to him like that, but the security was four to one. They'd throw him out and he definitely wanted to stay and have a good time. He wasn't drunk enough to know that an apology had to be made or else. It worked, they let him stay and he grinned.

Debbie went and got on the bike behind Tate, and she never let him know what had happened. He thought her shivering was due to the cold ride home. If she told him, he may want to go back, and try and whoop up on the oversize man. That would not be a good thing, he would probably beat Tate to a pulp.

Kirk was in town to have some fun, and he wanted female companionship which he found with a floozy, but he could not get the image of that feisty woman with the apron on out of his mind.

He'd settle up with her next time. She worked here, so there was no rush.

CHAPTER FIVE

Jason just turned seventeen and Marcus gave him bowling lessons as a gift. The bowling league was having a pro to mentor a child month. Marcus's friend, Jim Conway agreed to be Jason's mentor and teach him to bowl.

Marcus told Jason, "You learn how real good so you can teach me and your mom. Okay?"

The first day Jason was really bad, but so were the other teenagers that did not have a clue how to bowl. All their parents were well off, and he was going to be careful with whom he hung around because of the Charlie incident.

He was making a lot of friends that bowled every week, and played golf. That was something that Marcus liked to do. So maybe he could learn both. Marcus said in the winter stick with the bowling, and he would teach him golf in the summer. If his grades were good that was something to work toward, and Jason was applying himself in school. Now that he did not have to deal with that girl named Cheri.

The third bowling lesson he turned to go to the restroom and there she stood, smiling at him in her mini skirt and her tight sweater, and knee high boots. She was with her mother and maybe her brother. She had his attention that was for sure. She was walking toward him, and he was getting a funny feeling in the pit of his stomach. He was not going to move this time. She was not going to bully him, or throw herself at him in this crowd … he hoped.

She said, "Long time NO SEE." She was acting nice and polite. So he was staring back at her. It had been four years.

He said, "Yeah, it has been."

Cheri said, "Sorry about that year. I was going through a rebellious period. My parents were divorcing so I was doing everything I could to make them show me some attention. I used you to get back at them. Sorry!"

"I was really not expecting that to be the reason. I thought you thought I was good looking," he laughed and so did she.

Jim came by and said he had to get back to bowling and he did, "See ya!"

"If you're lucky!" and she left.

She was all he could think about the rest of the night. I got to talk to Corey again. His body was talking to him big time and he wanted to be prepared, or was it just wishful thinking.

She really was not giving him the time of day. Last time she was all over him, and she felt so good. He was more mature now. Right? He laughed at himself. Maybe he'd talk to Jim. Oh no, bad idea then he would tell Marcus. Best to suffer the growing pains alone.

The next lesson she was there, and she was bowling with the same woman and boy. When he went to the restroom, she did not appear. He was disappointed and went back and really bowled a good game. Every time he looked her way, she was staring and then looked away.

Jim asked, "Do you know that girl?"

Jason said, "Not really. We went to the same school several years back, that's all!"

"Her father just died, and the wife got remarried. She and the boy were not doing well until they started bowling. We are trying to help the mother by getting them to talk. So far its not working. Do you care if I ask them to bowl with us?"

"Fine by me," that is why she has changed. Her father died just like mine did. That was tough and he was little and his dad was his hero. So he'd try to be nice to her this time. He had the ups on her. She was the one that was hurting, not him.

Her mother introduced them and thanked Jim for asking. They played a couple of games. Cheri did not smile one time, and she was so bubbly and mischievous the last time at school, so he asked her.

"Are you okay?" Jason was truly concerned.

"I'm okay. Just don't know how to bowl. Why I have to come is beyond me," Cheri said looking at the front door. Like she wanted to run, "Can't leave my brother with her. I promised him, or I would be out that door so fast."

"How old's your brother?" he asked.

"Ten," she said and looked at her shoes. "Hideous shoes."

"That was about how old I was when my dad got kill. He was in the U.S. Army," he looked at his own bowling shoes and added, "They definitely are bad looking shoes."

She looked at him, "I'm sorry I didn't know about your dad. My dad overdosed," a tear ran down her face, and he handed her his napkin from his nacho tray.

"That's a bummer," Jason said. She said, "Yeah, it is."

Jim heard them talking and asked the mother and boy, if they wanted to get a drink. They left the two teenagers talking.

"It is something no one else, but my big brother Corey knows. How bad I was hurting. I didn't want to make my mother cry and she would, if I cried. So I wouldn't unless I was with Corey. Are you the one your brother comes to when he wants to cry?" Jason had to ask.

"Yeah! That is weird because you of all people know what I am going through." Cheri still had not looked at him.

"You can't hold it in. Let it out! I'm a good listener," Jason was hoping she would, but she wouldn't.

"Thanks. I have to share something else my mom doesn't know," Cheri stopped and looked at her mom. "I was stealing drugs from my dad. That is why I was so high the other year and did some WEIRD stuff. You are the only one that knows that. You don't go to my school anymore, so you won't tell anyone?"

"No ... I will not tell anything to anyone, but sharing means you trust me," and Jason smiled at her and tried to make her look at him.

Finally Cheri did, "I am so ashamed. I threw myself at you and you would not hold me or anything."

"I wanted to and you definitely did not want me to hold you the way my body was reacting," and he laughed.

She looked at him and burst out laughing. She smiled at him. Her mother came over and smiled at him.

Jason said, "It was a joke. I like to tell jokes. Sorry!"

"Don't be Cheri has a beautiful laugh. I just haven't heard it in a long time. Now let's bowl," and they all bowled and laughed for the next hour.

Cheri said, "Thanks Jason. Jeremy really enjoyed himself as did my Mom."

"You are welcome. Jim and I are here every Monday and Thursday bowling. Jim don't you think it would be okay, if they bowled with us again?"

"By all means," and Jim shook Jeremy's hand and Cheri's mom shook Jason's hand. Cheri did not shake anyone's hand, and it was okay because she was at least smiling.

Jason could hardly wait to talk to Corey and Corey told him to cool his heels. "If her mom is watching, you are not going to need condoms."

"I know but I want them just in case, you never know!" Jason did not care this year, if Cheri hit on him. Dang! He was now wishing she would. "No! Stop that!" he told himself.

"She has the prettiest eyes, Corey!" Jason said.

"That ain't what you said several years ago!" Corey was killing himself laughing. "What did I say?" Jason asked.

"You said she had the prettiest tits and she was rubbing them all over you. That's why you wanted to change schools. Remember?" and he popped him on the back of the head.

"Oh yeah! Now I remember!" Like he could EVER forget. Those had kept him up many nights. A TV station had a girl's tits her size and the other things. Mom blocked that station!

Roscoe talked to Guy, and he followed him home on his motorcycle, parked it, and got the car to bring Kyleigh and Madison home.

"Thank you Bro, for watching out for my family. Wish I could wrap them in a cocoon and keep them safe. Kyleigh loves the outdoors. I don't ever want her to lose that joy. Do you think we will all have to stay at Trevor's again?" asked Guy.

"Don't know, we have to talk to him? God I hope not. My seven will wreck the place. You all just come to my house!" Roscoe said and Guy shook his head, "To visit a couple hours is all I can take. I am use to the quiet!"

Roscoe laughed, "You are a whimp!"

"That's me! I get weak at the knees! Every time Kyleigh comes close to me. I ..." Guy was pouring it on.

"Oh shut up braggart! You always do that! What's wrong with you, Bro. You trying to twist my arm and make me tell you our secret. It's call a vasectomy. You can any time, where, how, and never worry again!" that was Roscoe triumphant speech.

"And it took you seven children later to figure that one out!Bravo Bravo!" Guy loved seeing Roscoe get frazzled.

"You are really getting on my nerves. GS my man, you are going to get your butt whooped. If you don't shut up!" Roscoe said now that they were at the house.

Both got out and high-fived each other, "Like old times!"

"Yep, it was. Kinda miss you Bro!" Guy said.

Roscoe walked on in and said, "Good!"

"I can't tell her. You tell her," Guy pleaded. Roscoe,"You!"

Beatrice and Kyleigh were sitting and talking while the kids were watching an educational program about animals and none were moving, just riveted to the movie screen.

Guy said, "This is amazing," and whispered in Kyleigh ear. "Can I see you outside for a moment," and waved to Roscoe.

"Honey get in the car! I have to take you to the house and ravish you there, or I have to ravish you in the car which do you prefer? I told Roscoe. He was okay with it either way."

She was striking him on the head.

"I was just kidding, Honey! Wow that turns me on. You are so forceful and strong," Guy said.

"Everything turns you on Guy. You have a one track mind!" Kyleigh said and laughed.

"And you have those skinny jeans on. That is really why we are going home for a few. For you to wiggle out of them and put something else on. Okay we are here! Hop to it woman!"

"Oh no, you didn't?" Kyleigh was furious.

Then he scooped her up and carried her inside, and all was forgiven. Then he told her about Michelle and the Hawaii ordeal, and having to move them to a safe house.

Kyleigh asked, "Can you move me to a safe house?"

"We can go to Trevor's, if you will feel safer?" Guy was so afraid something would happen to her and she was realizing it was HIS fear.

She kissed him and said, "We are going to be okay. Don't you worry." She had to reassured him and it gave her the power and control of the situation. It empowered her and he was happy his plan had worked. He called GM.

CHAPTER SIX

Madeline was preparing Michelle to be a red haired darling. "Honey you have had black hair, and blonde hair and it is high time for a switch to red. I went on line so we could have a fun day of dress up. To see which of them that you like the best, and which Robert likes best. Sound good?"

"As a little girl I never had a mother to play dress up with. It will be a dream come true. You are the mother that I always wanted. I will tell Robert to stay away until we call him," and she laughed because it was hard to keep him away.

Madeline had a tearful moment because she and Jo Ann, her daughter that was killed, had had many play days dressing up. Michelle just validated how special those days were to a small child, and a tear dropped on the wig.

It was a long, down the back red mahogany wig. She gave her amethyst "violet" eye contacts, and dressed her in a tunic with dark gray slacks. Three inch pointed toed dark gray shoes with matching Kenneth Hahn shoulder bag completed the outfit. "Wow!" Madeline gasped.

"You look just like a model, dear. Call Robert! And I will step out," Madeline eased out as Robert came flying around the corner and into the room.

He stopped and stared. He saw her, but he didn't see his Michelle. Just when he thought she could never get more desirable, here she stood proving him wrong.

She walked toward him and he looked into her violet eyes and then he saw his Michelle. She was the same delicious treat. He said, "Madeline is going to have to stay away from this room for awhile. Do you agree?" and she nodded.

He forgot to let her make that call. He devoured her mouth and pulled her onto his need.

She said, "I think this is a good look BUT Madeline has more to show me and you?"

He was enjoying this never ending climax, and she could not speak. He would not waste a minute of what they had on decisions. Finally they heard a knock at the door.

"I'll go in the bathroom," Robert stated. She had her robe on as if she was ready to try on something else.

"How did he like it?" Madeline could tell Michelle's face was flushed.

"He liked it but wants to see more as I do?" and she giggled which was not her usual laugh. "I'm trying to change my mannerisms as well."

Michelle tried on the dark auburn short wig that was short in the back and its sides dipped below her chin. She immediately put one strand of hair on one side behind an ear. Changed earrings to long teardrops, and donned a cashmere light green off the shoulder sweater. Pairing it with pale green pair of plaid trousers that had a side zipper that emphasized her tiny waist, and topping it off with palomino colored boots and a matching large clutch purse.

Her contacts this time were honey brown over her blue eyes. Madeline left, and Robert came out of the bathroom.

"Oh my wife … Look at you!" Staring into her eyes, "No one would be able to recognize you my Darling, but me and I have all the inside info in this brain of mine of my true Michelle. My sexy vixen I cannot stop the need to ravish you!

Promise me that we will always play dress up in the future?"

"You betcha! I mean. Yes, my dear husband. Got to switch to my new persona. Now GM has some more looks just for you! I am dying to see them," her new honey golden eyes of brown were boring a hole through his mindset.

"Go! Before we embarrass Madeline. I know what you are thinking Robert. Let me see you play dress up," and she gave him her devilish grin, and bit her lip.

"Oh I am going to play! Hold your thought," and out her door he went into the hallway. Madeline motioned for him to come into the bedroom next door.

"I appreciate all you are doing for us. If disguises is what it will take to keep her safe, I am all for it," he said sincerely.

Robert didn't say it was also heightening the intensity of their sex life as a bonus. He was really enjoying that added fringe benefit. Boy was he enjoying it, and looked at the ceiling to recover his senses.

Madeline gave him some gray contacts to go over his green eyes and a tiny goatee and longer sideburns. He donned a gray pinstriped double breasted suit, black wing-tip shoes and a black fedora.

"I started to get you a black umbrella, but I think that would be too much. You may want a black briefcase or do you have one?" GM laughed. "I am use to dressing Barbie, but never Ken. Forgive me. Now go show Michelle!"

He knocked on their bedroom door and she let him in. Her eyes grew to see him better, "Oh my frigging god!"

"Now that is NOT a lady's reaction, but I'll take it, Love." He turned and she patted and rubbed to make sure it was him and boy was it him.

"You sir, look good enough to dine on! Very tasty! Mighty tasty! Mister, what is your name?" Michelle grinned.

Later he said, "Madeline I think you have magical powers inside these disguises. Michelle says for you to work your hocus-pocus on me again!" Robert said with a devilish laugh.

GM grinned, "Well I have never seen you in blue jeans. These are blue stone-washed Levis. I have paired them with a brown Henley, and Ostrich cowboy boots with a suede brown Stetson. Then I got you a darker brown leather jacket tailored to give you room for the brown and blue plaid cowboy shirt with all those snaps. I hope you like it!"

Next on his upper lip, she put a sandy thick mustache that was the color of his own hair. His contacts were cobalt blue when he put them in.

She smiled, pleased with the results. She snapped her fingers and waved both her arms to one side in a drum roll. "VOILA!" He looked in the mirror and was shocked.

He walked up to the bedroom door and gave it a knock or two. He tipped his hat as Michelle answered, "Evening ma'am," and her mouth flew open.

"Damn!' as her eyes devoured every detail of his transformation. "I mean you look very very handsome cowboy!"

"I can't believe it is you under there! Let me check!"

Because of the heels on the boots, she had to stretch her arms a little bit further than usual, and he lifted her so she could kiss his mustache thoroughly.

He kicked the door shut.

"I'd recognize you by only one thing and there it is, Honey. Please take that hat off," she said and he threw it as he locked the door. "How about the boots?" he asked.

"Nah ... leave them on. I'm in a hurry!"

He canceled all his lectures for the year and told his staff to continue publishing his book until he returned. Their paychecks were guaranteed, and that he could not say where he was going.

"NO ONE and I mean no one is to give anyone out any of this information. Even if they say they are government or plane manufacturers. NOBODY! Is that clear?" he stated.

Affirmative was heard from all his employees.

Shocked as they were his editor-in-chief and his lawyer said, "I assure you that this must be of the utmost importance probably an undercover operation. He will tell us about it when he returns. Until then, do your jobs!"

Robert had Trevor take him to the bank, and he withdrew a large sum of money, and put it in his inside coat pocket that had a hidden zipper. They may need things and no one would have to fund them. As soon as they had their new names, and IDs, he could open a new account wherever!

The agents were moving them tonight, and it was as before not specified where that would be, nor what their new names would be. It did not matter to them as long as they were together, and as long as Jung was in prison. He was not going to stop until he killed her and she KNEW it.

She was slowly making Robert see how every day and every minute counted, and that they would not waste their life on the mundane. She was sad that she could not design, but he was giving up a great deal, also. His lecturing was what he had always worked toward. He told her that she meant more than anything in THIS world.

"We will explore other options that we have always wanted to do. It will be challenging, but ever since I meant you in that cafe … you have been a challenge. I love a good challenge!" he grinned and kissed her.

"I am worth it. Wouldn't you say?" and she threw her head back and laughed.

"You are so worth it! I will make you happy, my Michelle. I promise. Never doubt it. This is what I want. To be with my wife every day and night of my life," hugging her. They looked out the window at the sun going down setting behind the mountains.

He was going to miss these mountains.

"One day we will build a house near here. There is a clearing across from here that I've been eyeing daily. Would you like that?" Robert was serious and anxious for her answer.

He saw a tear fall, "I would love that … but it will never be possible."

"All things are possible in love and war. I am declaring war on all the people that mess with my dreams and the dreams of my wife."

She had no idea of the many military aviators and five star generals that was friends with Robert, and some were his colleagues. They had always said, "If ever you need anything, just give me a call."

If he had to, he was going to call in some of those favors. He would do it her way for awhile, and then make up his mind. This was just a small vacation from the day to day hassles of his stressful career.

To keep her safe was his first priority, and this sudden necessity to relocate had taken him by surprise.

They packed and talked. No sleep would come to them and the fear of the unknown brought back the heart wrenching loss of Haruto. Her last safe house was sad and heartbroken. She had focused on the words of Madeline, "Don't let it be for naught. We love you!"

This time was different. She was taking love with her and leaving the family she loved behind, but they will be safer without her. Their safety meant the most. This family had given so much to help her, she thought looking at Robert.

"One day I am going to pay them back!" Michelle vowed.

Robert said, "All they want is your love, Darling!"

"They have always had that!" and she snuggled closer into his arms as he stared out into the darkest of night.

CHAPTER SEVEN

The security around the lake was tight and no need to move everyone to Madeline and Trevor's. Trevor had announced via TEXTING them all. "Boy, am I getting good at this!"

"Yes dear. You are good at a lot of things. Now text them they can come anytime they want ... that the house is almost empty. Then put a sad emoji" she said.

"A what?" Trevor thought it sad that he didn't know.

"A sad face instead of a smiley face. All the faces are different. Want to pick one for me?" Madeline was teasing.

"Does it have one for COME HERE? If so put it on my phone," and Trevor smiled and pulled at her ponytail.

"OK, it is done?" he looked at his phone and she was walking away. He press the face and she said, "My phone is ringing," and ran to the house to get it.

"OMG! I have created an emoji that I may regret," she was walking toward him.

He was continuously pressing the 'come here' button.

"That's it! I will have to take your toy away!" She stood with her hand out.

"No way! This is my business phone and you are my business!" he put his phone in his pants pocket.

She walked away and he was fuming, "You mean you are not going to try and retrieve that EMOJI thing? Jeepers what has a guy got to do to get a little action around here?"

"Get dressed up," she said and went into the house. She walked back in the house and walked by Michelle and Robert's room, and was sad.

Jana came by her and hugged her, "I miss her too, already!"

Bruce gave his mom a hug, "She's going to be fine, MAMA BEAR!" That was the first time he had made reference to something … she and he … had shared when he was a little boy.

They would sit at his father Sam 's desk, and say Sam was the Papa bear, and that Madeline was the Mama bear.

She gave him a hug and walked to the kitchen, "Debbie what are we cooking tonight?"

Debbie said, "Trevor is getting dressed up and said he is taking his woman out to dinner tonight!"

Madeline put her hand over her mouth and laughed, "OH MY GOD! I guess I had better be getting dressed up, too!"

They all knew what a treat it was for them two to get out of the house. Madeline was not going to tell Trevor what she meant by getting dressed up, and would save that for another day.

She showered and pulled her hair up into a pile of dangling curls and put on her Versace blue gown with silver Jimmy Choo heels and clutch to match.

She added her diamond and sapphire earrings and ring, extra makeup with baby blue eye shadow, and curled her lashes with a black mascara wand.

She would definitely be batting them tonight. It took her a total of thirty minutes, and she sat waiting for him by the fire.

"Is this dressed up enough?" He had his black tux on with his white shirt and bola tie. This was special because he even had his black cowboy boots on.

Now she felt like Michelle mentally devouring her man in his disguise. She smiled, and he had no clue why her eyes were sparkling. "I guess YOU are saying without saying it that I need to dress up more often," Trevor concluded.

"No darling! Just ever once in a while I think we should because I like my jeans and cowboy boots TOO much!" They were comfortable with their everyday attire, and left all the fancy dressing up back in Dallas until tonight.

They put on the outer finest wraps and James drove them to THE CASINO. A private dining area in the back had been set aside for just him and her. There was a man playing the baby grand piano. Soft classic hits with a Frank Sinatra like voice crooning, "I did it my way!" and "It had to be you!"

"This is a good thing my darling. I am glad you suggested it. It brings back memories. Fond memories of the days when I got a dance or two with you, but I could do nothing but dance with you." Trevor whispered.

"Tonight you can replace those memories. We can do anything your little heart desires," Madeline purred and batted those eyelashes.

"You do that again and we won't be eating here," and he grinned.

"What are we having tonight, Trev? Madeline inquired.

"We are having dress up night. You did really good with dressing up Michelle and Robert. I could not have recognized them in a crowd, but in my house I did process of elimination and bingo instantly knew my Michelle. Robert, by his height.

Tonight we celebrate their new life. Champagne?" he asked.

"Martini, please. My habits are hard to break," and she placed her hand on his.

He ordered her a martini and his usual brandy, and they got up to dance. He swung her around the small room in a slow dance that would have made DWTS proud.

Marcus and Eunice joined them. They were also having a dress up night, and it was good to have friends that they could celebrate with. Michelle loved to spend time with the Buchanans while she lived here these past four years at Southfork.

"Corey and Ellen have gone bowling with Jason tonight. So when Trevor called, I asked Adam and Janice, and they are going to the movies, so here we are! I know you two are going to miss that girl!"

"We needed to get out of the house and dress up. Didn't we Eunice? Yes, I will miss them both!" Madeline declared.

With her champagne glass she held it high Eunice said, "Here! Here!" Her Vera Wang was stunning in pastel pink with a pink diamond brooch on her right shoulder.

Touching her hand to it, Eunice asked, "Didn't he do good for our Fourth anniversary present?" she kissed his cheek.

Marcus was smiling and loosening his tie, "She makes me hot under the collar." They all were laughing hysterically by the time the food was served.

It was almost midnight when they got home.

Adam and Janice were dressed in jeans and were eating popcorn and smooching in the movie room. They had the entire mansion to frolic in.

"Why in the world would we want to go to a dinky old theater to go to the movies? When we have this whole beautiful house to romp in!" Janice stated.

"Are you sure my precious wife?" giving her his sexiest smile and holding her and rubbing her sweet little round belly.

It had taking them four years of rigorous sexual encounters to make this MIRACLE happen.

"We have to make all our wild fantasies come true now because in five months we are going to be the most respectable parents this town has ever seen," that was one of Adam's goals.

He had not had parents that cared. This child was going to have parents that shared their hearts everyday. Making him or her the best little person that they could be.

Family had become Janice's salvation. Her accident had put her priorities in order and Adam was the best thing that had ever happened to her. His family was a loving family.

He had shared his past with her, and said he was not worthy of her. That is when he excelled in his job, and now owned his own repair shop and their business was booming.

She had told him after she had recovered from the wreck that the baby was Justin's, and figured he would turn on her.

He said, "It was meant to be. I will never hold that against you. You were sent to me to save my life. I love ALL of you!"

"If the baby had lived, I would have loved it as my own. So don't ever feel you trick me. I felt I tricked you by not telling you MY past, which was way worst." It really had taken a burden off his and her chest. Honesty made them stronger.

That chest that she was rubbing right now was so so muscular, and toned from hard work. She was aching for him to fill her soul with ecstasy.

Their lovemaking had never dwindled, it had only grown in magnitude. He nor she never took it for granted. They tried to make each night as if it was the first time. The time and effort was what made the fireworks explode in the air.

She grinned at him. He was not believing it, she wanted him. She was wiggling that finger and it was on. Pregnancy had been a blessing because she didn't have to hold back anything.

Trying to lose weight to look good was a thing of the past. He would worry her and say you are suppose to be getting bigger. Just those compliments made him more appetizing to her. She could eat him alive, and she tried to every chance that she got.

She was in her exercise group today and they were doing pelvic thrust to strengthen muscles, and she almost had an organism thinking about him and about tonight.

She was showing him her new exercise moves.

He said, "Wait right there, Girly," and he stripped down. "Now do that move again. He was moaning and she was moaning. Over and over, they rocked their own world.

It had been six months that Jason had been bowling, and he was bowling strikes tonight. Cheri was cheering him on. Her mother nor brother were here tonight. She was bouncing around like he use to remember. It had taken her all this time to open up.

Cheri was smiling at him, "That was excellent. You are the best!"

It was her turn and she got a split and pretended pouting. Pouting was another thing she never did, but tonight she wanted him to put his arms around her and tell her it was alright. That is something, he had started doing. His comforting was weighing on both of their nerves.

He did hug her quickly. "It's okay. You will get a strike next time." Since it was not a tournament game, he could slack off and let her win.

He walked her to her car. "Come sit with me!" and patted the seat. He got in, but he was not going to be able to sit long.

Then she said, "We talk about everything," and she smiled.

"I have to ask why have you not kissed me?" Cheri was staying to her side of the car. He was sitting on his door handle on the opposite side.

"I am afraid to," he just put it out there.

"Jason, I won't break," she rubbed his cheek.

"I know, but I am not prepared," he really was and had had a condom in his wallet for a whole year. Hoping it would not expire. He laughed.

"Prepared for what?" she was shocked.

"I am not prepared to stop when it comes to you, and it terrifies me," he said.

"Explain that one to me?" she shook her head.

"MY sister was gang raped. I am told and the thought that I may not be able to stop making love to you terrifies me."

There it was, and he stared into her eyes.

"So you are saying you want to make love to me. Is that what you are saying?" she looked down. She was so shy without the drugs influencing her brain.

Then she looked up.

"Yes, I respect you and I want you something terrible. I have trouble sleeping because that is all I can think about at night," Jason was looking out the window.

"I have trouble sleeping thinking about you doing the same to me." There it was, Cheri had said it.

"What do you want to do about it?" he asked.

"I want you, but I want a ring of promise first," she said.

"That sounds fair," but he was swelling at just the prospect.

"When do you want to pick it out," Jason was in pain.

Cheri rubbed his arm and held his hand, "Tomorrow!"

"Can I kiss you?" he asked pleading.

"Tomorrow," he was so close to her mouth.

"You know and I know that is not possible here in the parking lot with all these parents that will call our parents."

"Tomorrow I will pick you up after school. I have no classes after twelve, so call me when you want me."

Jason begged, "Not even one little kiss?"

"No," she said firmly.

That night he asked Corey for two more condoms, and his eyes got so big.

"Jason what in the hell are you planning an orgy?" Corey must do some talking and talking fast to his little brother.

"You told me to be safe and prepared. I am getting engaged tomorrow, and I am hoping I am rewarded," and he grinned.

"Where are you getting the money for a ring?" Corey asked.

"I have been saving and if it is not enough, can I borrow some?" Jason was not going to Marcus.

If he had to, he would.

"You know Mom wants you to go to college," Corey stated.

"I can go like you and be married. So don't give me that!" Jason had a point.

"OK. Just let me know. I'll go get them now!" He went to his room and Ellen was there and saw Corey with a handful of condoms.

"OK who is she?" she knew he could not possibly have anyone on the side with what they did every night and grinned at him.

"I want the Bro to have protection and he is asking a girl to marry him tomorrow! I think it is that Cheri that has been driving him crazy for five years. I FORGOT to ask."

"Daggone it!" Corey grabbed her and kissed her. "I know you drove me crazy. I was lucky you were on the pill. I would never have … never been able to get a condom on!" he said and then she laughed.

CHAPTER EIGHT

Roscoe and Beatrice were stepping out for the night. He was escorting her to THE INN for a meal away from his seven athletic children ranging from the oldest twins, Cain and Caleb twelve. They were into baseball and were the XBOX champions of the town. He laughed.

The twin girls, BeBe and FiFi were eleven and into shopping and volleyball tournaments ... his little darlings.

Lastly the triplets were ten and the boy, Johnny was a tag-along for his big brothers as a water boy for their baseball team. He was getting a throwing arm though. If Cain and Caleb didn't watch out, the little brother might become their pitcher. He was getting long legs at ten and his height was reaching the twelve year old's height. Roscoe thought wouldn't that be something.

"Three on the same team," and he was beaming.

The triplet girls, Jill and Jessie were tomboys and football was their favorite. Yes, FOOTBALL! They became cheer-leaders after years of gymnastics. Finally they had curbed their tomboy ways into tumbling for the team.

"Like a girl, Yuck!" Jill said.

"Double Yuck! But daddy said it was a tough sport. So we are tough and will give it a try!" said Jessie.

They high-fived just like the boys and then chest-bumped, since they had no chest. They made Roscoe proud.

He looked at the pale green-eyed beauty beside him and said, "Let's take the Silverado instead of that van?"

"Okay, Mr. Lucky!" Beatrice said.

"Don't do that with those gorgeous legs. We will never make it to the restaurant!" he said. She propped her egg shell white legs across his lap like she use to do.

"Complain! Complain!" Beatrice smiled.

"This could be hazardous to my health," Roscoe frowned.

"Driving under the influence, I could get arrested. Stop! I'm a married man," then Roscoe grinned at her.

"Just like old times, Mister. Always living on the edge for you and I. Honey, sugar, baby of mine! Are you really hungry?" Beatrice asked biting her bottom lip.

"Oh yes. Yes, I am starving! You wanna?" Roscoe asked.

"You know it," she responded by taking her shoes off and climbing into that big backseat.

He whipped into their favorite lover's lane on the side of the interstate that was always deserted. For years it was their, 'get out of the house and go crazy' place.

"Everyone should have a place like this. I hope they never excavate that mountain, and put an excess road through here. Then we will be out of luck," Roscoe rubbed her legs.

"You are Mr Lucky! What a thing to say... do you actually think we could not find another love cove in this neck of the woods?" she unzipped him.

"You have got a point there. Boy, do you have a point and people actually go out to eat on date night! What are they thinking?" he nuzzled her ear and lifted her dress.

"Definitely not what you and I are thinking," Beatrice said.

Jason went and picked Cheri up in the Jeep that Marcus brought him for his sixteenth birthday, two years ago. It was the ride that he liked then, but he had to help her in that was the problem and her boots had slick bottoms.

She had on tight jeans with boots and the boots were making her slip off the step under the door... Or was she doing it on purpose? He sure was getting a good feel.

"Do you want to help me or your mother is going to kill me? RIGHT here in your driveway!" her driveway was steep and he was definitely keeping his back to the house.

When he got in, she was grinning. "I think you like me! Or do you have a banana in your pocket?"

"Do you like bananas?" he asked. Two could play at this game. He said, "And I happen to love you."

Cheri had never heard him say it, and she swallowed the teasing. Saying, "I love you too, Jason very much and always have," her eyes got misty.

"Don't you dare do that! It is a happy day for us and where do you want to go first?" he asked and drove toward town.

They went by several jewelry stores, and she finally found what she wanted. "Are you sure?" he asked.

She said, "Yes I am." He got down on one knee and asked, "Will you marry me, Cheri?"

"I will, if you get up and pay the man," and he kissed her quickly and walked outside.

"That was not a good kiss Jason," she was disappointed.

"I did not want to have a boner in the store or we can go back in, and I will tickle your tonsils," they both laughed.

She got in the Jeep real fast this time because he had lifted his coat and proven he was not lying.

"I was going to help you get in. Dang! I missed out on that one," and he laughed.

"If it got any bigger, we would never hear the end of the gossips. You know we have to tell my mother and your mom before they do," she stated the facts.

"Not like this, I got to have some relief and you said quote if I have a ring on it?" He was pushing it, but had to be up front with her.

"I need you bad and I have protection," Jason was begging and she was thinking.

"But where?" Cheri asked.

"On the mountain," he had thought it through and through.

"I am on the pill, so throw those away. You had better not need them," Cheri was smiling at Jason.

"I want you, too!" she said.

"OH crap! You had to say that when I'm in the middle of traffic," Jason frowned.

"Well pull over," she took her hand and placed it on his hand and brought it over to her crotch.

His mouth flew open and he almost ran off the road. The next park bench, he pulled over. No one was around and he got out and walked around the other side, and she was waiting for him to slide her out. She unzipped and he unzipped and her wetness took him by surprise and he was done. He said," I am so so so sorry."

"We will go on up the mountain and it will be good for you. I know I will make it good for you," Jason groveled.

"Who said it wasn't good for me?" she had him around the neck and he was closing his eyes as she fitted him into the most wonderful place yet.

"You see now. Why ... I couldn't come near you for five years?" Jason stated firmly.

"I am so sorry that I put you through it! I just didn't know!"

"We both learned something today. I can't live without you! I want what we have forever!" he pledged his love.

For two hours, they were making up for five years of want. Four years of need and it was worth the wait.

When they finally came to their senses and realized it soon would be dark, and the woods wasn't a place they should be.

They drove by a service station and stopped.

The one toilet was outside. They were laughing and he said, "I don't know how I will live without you now?"

"What do you mean live without me?" Cheri was puzzled.

"I mean, I want you with me every night for the rest of my life and I am already dying to have you again," he was kissing her and she said, "We have to go!"

"Those men were looking at me weird?" Cheri said.

"You are right! We have to go, and they weren't looking at you. They were looking at my thing. Like they would like to chop it off," and she started laughing. Jason made her laugh and he made her feel loved. She looked at her ring. It was not big or expensive, but it was what he could afford without asking his family for money and that meant a lot to her.

"Jason I do love you and I am glad, we waited. You are eighteen, and I will be in a few days, so let's get married. If you want, and we don't have to tell anyone. It can be our secret."

"No," he said.

"You don't want me?" she gasped.

"I want you to have the wedding you deserve," he said.

"That can take months and months to plan and cost a lot of money," she said.

They were almost at her house.

"You are right. We can have a big one later on," he said.

"I'll come in if you want me to, but I can't come near you or kiss you without it going haywire again," he added.

She kissed him and said, "Go! We will figure it out tomorrow or the day after," she walked into her house and shut the door.

Corey meet him at the door. "I threw them away. Sorry?" Jason said.

"What do you mean you threw them away?" Corey asked.

"She's on the pill," and Jason kept walking until he found Marcus and Eunice.

"Mom and Dad I just ask Cheri to marry me, and I gave her a ring," and he walk out and up to his room.

"You got balls!" Corey said and high-fived him, "and lock your door!"

He did and went to sleep for an hour. He was tired and so relaxed, and he laughed. He called her and they talked till midnight, and they had exams soon.

No way was he going to be able to concentrate on tests.

Corey said, "If I can do it. You can do it. Remember we were quarantined to Trevor's, and Ellen was driving me crazy. Well WE got married and everything worked out. They are not going to throw you out. So do it legal, and bring her on home. It is not like you don't have closet space for her."

Marcus knocked on his door. "Your mother is upset. She wants you to finish school and go to college."

"I am going to marry her and soon. I want it to be with you 'all blessing. I can go to school and work let Tate and Corey. It is no sense in getting a girl pregnant and dropping out of school. That would have Mom more upset."

"Is she pregnant, son?" Marcus asked.

"No, unless it happened a couple hours ago and her birth control pills didn't work. I didn't touch her until after I gave her the ring and ask her to marry me. I SWEAR," Jason wanted Marcus to believe that he had thought it through like a man.

"You called me Dad and now I 'm going to act like one. If you want to get married, then I will take you to get the license. If she wants a big wedding it will take awhile."

"I know that is what she says months and months. I can't wait that long. I will never be able to concentrate on my exams. The sooner the better, I will never forget this, if you help me. I really need your help. When I get a job, I'll pay you back." Jason was laying it on thick, knowing all the while that Marcus wouldn't want him to pay him back.

Cheri was talking to her mother and showing her the ring.

"He loves me and wants to get married now. Can you sign for me?"

"You will be marrying into a rich family, of course I will. I want my baby to be well taken care of. Jason is a nice boy and I have watched him help you get yourself back together, and thank God you are on the pill. So people will not talk afterward that you are pregnant. You have to finish school promise me that!"

"I will! I will! I love you mother!" and she hugged her. She went into her bedroom and called Jason, and he told her what Marcus had said.

"How about tomorrow!" he asked.

She squealed, "What time?"

PART TWENTY

CHAPTER ONE

Michelle was now Jasmine married to John. The Waynes were settling into Montana away from the busy streets. They were renting a farmhouse with their own money and he purchased two horses, a quarter horse for him and a pinto for her.

She did not know one thing about a horse. This was something that he wanted to teach her. He had always rode and occasionally participated in a polo match or two. His college buddies included him in all their activities because he was a "chick" magnet.

They patted him on the back and said, "Robert you will never get married. If you did, we would have no fun!"

They would be so surprised to know that he was having more fun now, than he ever did with them. He seldom saw them, and he had some new adventure everyday, a continuous love-fest with his wife.

Just looking at her outside the window made him throb.

Here she could paint, and he could work on new gadgets for the planes that he had built, and now serviced. Something he had on his bucket list, but never had time to do.

They cleaned out the horse stalls and he grabbed her and sat her on a bale of hay. "Are you happy, my love?" he asked.

"Extremely happy! I will race you to the top of the loft." She made sure, she climbed slowly up the ladder preventing him from going around her. Her derriere was brushing his cheek and she wiggled it to make him moan.

"Sorry my climbing days are not what they use to be!" What a lie. She could climb Everest, if it was to get to him. Jasmine put her hands in her jeans and lowered her head like she was exhausted.

"Don't give me that woe is me. Remember I know you. Others you can pull that stunt on but..." John lifted her head so she was staring him in the face.

"You have the stamina of ten racehorses," he grinned.

She on tiptoe, bit his lip, as her arms went around his neck.

"And don't you ever forget it! My horse engine is revving up. Do you think you can keep up?" Slowly she unbuttoned his shirt, then she fiercely yanked it out of his Levis.

"OH my girl wants to play rough today?" he drew her to him and gave her a rough and deep kiss while holding her head with one hand, and holding her buttocks firmly with the other.

"Okay," she said to herself, "I will play the weakling this time. Sometimes this weak facade brings strong rewards."

"Oh baby you are so forceful! I don't know if I can take it all," and she whimpered.

"The hell you say! Don't play innocent. Innocence will get you a spanking," John laughed.

"Promises, promises!" Jasmine went too far.

Her flannel shirt had come open and he turned her across his knee and spanked her.

She raised her head and looked back at him, her nipple touched his leg, "Harder harder. Spank me harder!" and squeezed her legs around his arm.

He flipped her over and stared into her violet eyes, "Okay You want it harder. You got it!" He could not let her win this one.

Play the part, he told himself. But he could not play the part of throwing her down. He laid her down softly, so she could see what she was getting as he unbuckled. She began smiling and bucking up, smiling and closed her eyes.

With straw in her hair she rose to lick his lips, and he just stood there like a statue. She would break him down. He knew it and she knew it.

"I said harder," as she shed her jeans and placed her right pointed toes near as she could to his right shoulder. "A Ballet Split! On the floor is no comparison to the this. Put it in cowboy, and hold me tight that I will wish that I had said more, instead of harder."

This was her fantasy and "oh my" was she the tightest this way, and he went slow. It took his breath away. She was moaning and he was loving it. Just to see her face, did him in.

Her hands were locked behind his neck as he pulled her buttocks back and forth. She was helping him remain stable.

He asked, "Harder cowgirl?" and stamina was taking over.

"Damn you are killing me! No No amount of comparison!This is the best! Now baby!" They climaxed while he continued to hit her G-spot." They crumpled to floor, lifeless.

Floyd was laying across the counter in his service station talking to Ferguson. Did you see them two teenagers go in the bathroom? Motel 6, that's what it is Floyd. Your bathroom!"

"Yep! Last month it was that teacher with the most beautiful geisha, I ever seen. Ferguson do you think they are on to us?"

"Don't get your dandruff up about those kids? I saw his thing and he wasn't any NARC agent. He was getting him some WHOOPEE. Wish you 'd knock a hole in the wall!"

"Go to the movies Ferguson. Every one of them got what's in my bathroom on the screen, Maggot! Have you seen Glen? He is late with his pick up today!" and Floyd spit his tobacco juice in the cup as he asked.

He called Ferguson ... Maggot ... because he was rotten to the core.

"He 'll be on in a few. Don't get yourself in a stew. That principal is in SO deep he needs thigh-high waders." Ferguson had seen the amount of dope that principal had picked up from Floyd this month.

Floyd 's was the drop off place for this neck of the mountains. Charlotte and Mebane were the other two.

Floyd chuckled, "Thanks Ferguson. I need a kick in the butt every now and then."

Ferguson asked, "How's the wife?" Floyd got the stash for his wife. It eased her cancer pain so he did worry, if the shipment was late.

"She's good. She don't rip my noggin' off any more!" Floyd took his baseball cap off and scratched his head and put it back on. "Thanks for everythin' Maggot!"

Ferguson was a dealer and Glen was a seller for the upper crust in the community.

All their fancy parties, they needed to invite the principal every time. Glen had said, "That's what private schools are for ... to keep everything private!" and he would laugh.

Floyd was not fond of him, "Sho enuf don't like his type!"

Two hours later, Glen came rushing in babbling about a school meeting delaying him. He was red in the face and sniffling.

Ferguson said, "You been dipping in the profits, Mr Glen?

You know I'll cut your balls off, if I find out." He walked away from Glen and up to Floyd 's counter and paid for his drink.

"Nothin' I like any better'n than castratin' a HOG! Floyd just keep me filled in," he nodded and left on his semi-truck, a huge Peterbilt.

Drugs were paying for his truck that was all he cared about, paying for his ride. It had a bed in it, refrigerator and stove, "What mor' a man needs?" he told himself as he pulled out into the highway and onto his next stop.

Floyd's nephew a big burly lumberjack by the name of Kirk Matterhorn stopped by the station for a pick up, also.

"Been a month where ya been! Wat's up?" Floyd was still leaning over the counter.

"Got in a fight! Been in the pokey for a few days. Need to pick up and go, Unc." Floyd got him what he was after, and shook his head. Never were they close enough for a hug. The kid didn't even ask about his own aunt.

Bruce was scouting the town to see, if he saw any faces that he recognized. Jana went with him to do his community service for the court. She helped to serve the meals.

While at the homeless shelter, he did recognize a drug dealer. Moses was no longer dealing, if he was in a place like this. Bruce took him a plate of food, and sat with him.

"Hey man, how are you doing?" Bruce needed to get some info from him. For a price, he could get anything from this man because of his habit. He would do anything for Bruce. Bruce had saved him twice from being killed. He had told Moses "three times and you're out!"

Bruce had never wanted the LOW man on the totem pole. The masterminds and kingpins took years to infiltrate their organizations. Those are who he wanted still. Unitus and he missed it. He had to get a message to the underground that would spread like wild fire. It could solve a major problem. He needed to at least try.

"Can you do me a favor?" Bruce slipped him a fifty under the pie plate.

"Of course. Anything for my main man," Moses was shoveling the food in as he talked.

"Put it out there … the RAVEN has flew the coop. The Porter house is clear! Thanks man. I am here twice a week, if you hear anything about where she is? See ya!" Bruce said.

"Not if I see you first!" that was their standard goodbye phrase. He took the money and hide it in his sock. He would do it for Bruce. He was a good man.

Moses was found dead in the alley the next morning.

When Bruce read the paper, HOMELESS man found with throat slashed. His jaw clinched. Jana saw it. Bruce would never go to that shelter again. He did not want Jana going with him ever again. Even though she enjoyed it so much, it was not safe. She read his mind.

If someone was just going to rob Moses, they would have knocked him in the head, not killed him. If they wanted to send Bruce a message, then they'd do this.

This was the normal way for the drug cartel. It was the "DEATH message. The YOU are next buddy!"

He was going to have to fight for the family. If he left, it would leave all the family vulnerable. If they put him back in jail, same difference. He had to talk to Unitus and Trevor, Roscoe and Guy.

This was family business. Bruce was under court order, maybe Adriana could get it lifted for a few days for him to do his former job. Only he did not have the CIA to back him now, but Trevor did.

He would not sit still this time. It was personal.

CHAPTER TWO

Marcus and Eunice went with Jason and Cheri, and her mother and stepfather to the Justice of the Peace. Corey and Ellen took pictures with their cell phones.

Marcus, Corey and Jason wore black tuxes. Eunice had insisted. Eunice wore a simple purple dress which was Jason's favorite color and she had pinned his father's military war MEDAL to the boy's tux upper pocket.

Cheri was dressed in a white simple jersey short dress with a silver waist belt that sparkled, and a pearl necklace that her FATHER had given to her mother, hung around her neck. Her mother said it was to be past down the family line.

She held a bouquet of violets since purple was Jason's favorite. Now purple was her fave, also.

It took fifteen minutes and he kissed the bride and held her in front of him smiling. The pictures were so good, and they would start a wedding album tomorrow.

Tonight everyone was at Trevor and Madeline's for a big BASH to celebrate the wedding of this special couple.

Trevor and the boys had met earlier and said they would tell everyone after the celebration to pick their rooms, and that no one could leave. The SBI and FBI were on their way to their previous assigned station, and Lonestar was here.

This was once again serious.

Bruce and Unitus were talking about Moses that was all it took for them to get into combat mode. This was war!

Marcus convince Trevor that his family would be safe at their fortress and the army of guards that he had at the mansion. He had doubled.

So they loaded up and left with an entourage of security.

Jason and Cheri were the most grateful to be going home for their first night as husband and wife.

Marcus was head of the family and made everyone feel safe. Eunice said, "Isn't he wonderful!" and he hugged her to his side.

Adriana was with her Unitus, and Angel who thought it great that she had Beatrice's girls to play with. The mighty Vanderbilt was getting passed around and held till Unitus said, "Boy is he going to have a good set of lungs. He's four! They're still holding him," eyeing Adriana who was not laughing.

Adriana stared at Unitus and said, "Please stay put for me!" he did not look at her.

"This is family!" and he joined Bruce and Trevor and Lonestar.

Roscoe and Guy were getting their families settled in for the long haul. It was taking a toll on Kyleigh, "I can't believe this!"

"Darling enjoy the family and Madison is having a ball roughhousing with Roscoe's crew. Those tomboys maybe a problem for him. They are getting too big to wrestle?" He wanted to divert her thought process for a little while.

"Yeah, I can take them out by the woodpile, if I have to!" Kyleigh laughed hysterically.

"Oops, too late Madison has just given Jessie a bloody nose.

Dang! He is a fighter. Like his daddy!" Guy said.

Roscoe walked by with an ice pack, "I have you know that was a Kyleigh punch. K ... I have seen you give GS one of those in the past."

"OH MY GOSH! I do remember," Kyleigh grinned at Guy.

"It was third grade."

Guy told Roscoe, "Mind your own business!" and frowned.

Roscoe said, "You are my business, Bro!" and walked away grinning.

She rubbed his nose and kissed it, "Madison is going to be really tired tonight! I bet he sleeps all night long!"

Guy's frown turned to a smile, "Are you going to sock me in the nose again?" He was trying to feel her legs even in third grade. Funny how you remember important things.

"Maybe! We'll see what happens, if you behave yourself?"

"Me ... or you talking to me?" Guy pointed to himself.

"I am always the gentleman and he sat closer, and due to the fullness of her party dress no one could see him working his hand up her leg, and she doubled over, "Don't stop! It is feeling real good," she said. Guy was shocked.

That was not the response, he wanted to hear in this crowded room. His eyes were widening because Kyleigh was so wet. She climbed over to sit in his lap. He was dying.

Roscoe walked by and gave him the thumbs up, and he gave him the index finger. Guy would truly get him back.

"Mercy! Kyleigh I have never had a lap dance! Can we do this in our room! Please get two of Madison's big toys for me to take to our room. BIG TOYS, honey! Thank you!" he dare not move.

"Please don't let Madison come over here!" he added.

Roscoe walked by again just to be a nuisance, "Something wrong Bro? Come here and tell me your problem!"

Guy said, "This problem will be solved soon and yours will only be starting," and he smiled because Kyleigh was back.

"Say goodnight to Roscoe, Honey!" Guy said as he navigated the toys toward their bedroom.

"Night Roscoe, "Kyleigh walked swaying those hips in front of Guy when he stopped to let her pass.

"Night Bro," and Guy blew him an air kiss since Kyleigh was holding one of the toys.

Roscoe caught it and threw it on the floor and stomped it and twisted his foot into the carpet, and gave Guy the index finger as he walked off.

His twin girls said, "That's right daddy we are number one!"

"It must be the champagne Guy. I am as loose as a goose," Kyleigh was stripping like she was pouring a cup of coffee.

She turned. He was frozen to the spot and she said, "Do I have to undress you, too?" and she rubbed up against him.

"You are DRUNK! I will be with you in a minute," and he stripped. Smiling he asked, "Can I get my lap dance again? I really did enjoy it!" kissing her shoulders as she sat down and gyrated. He closed his eyes and said, "one thousand, nine hundred ninety nine, nine hundred oh my word ... Honey!"

He grabbed her. They fell on the bed, just in time to finish.

"Wasn't that wonderful, Honey? I can't have any more champagne or I might want to..." she whispered in his ear.

Guy got a bottle of leftover champagne and sat it on the breakfast table. He looked at Kyleigh and grinned.

Madison said, "Can I have some ginger ale daddy?"

"This is not ginger ale, son. I will get you some."

"Guard that with your life K!" and he gave her the Groucho jumping eyebrows.

"OK but hurry. I am awful thirsty!" she smiled sweetly and batted her eyelashes.

Roscoe said, "You may not live to reach and old age Bro!"

Guy said, "I know. You are right. She is going to kill me tonight. See that bottle of champagne sitting beside her."

Roscoe was buttering his toast and Guy said, "She gave me lap dances all night long. Yes, that is what it does to her!" he grinned up at Roscoe who had just sliced his finger and didn't even know it.

Guy wrapped it with a napkin and said, "I told you I was going to get you back, but I had no idea you were going to hurt yourself! BUCK UP! Snap out of it! Beatrice your husband cut his finger. Help him! I got to eat my breakfast so I will have the strength to ..." He bit into his bagel and walked toward Kyleigh and Madison with a cup of ginger ale, smiling back at Roscoe.

The two of them through the years had played every trick in the book on each other. Some, that were not even in the book.

"I do love being in the same house with him, and GM and everyone else, but especially Roscoe. Brotherly love will make you STRONG! You have to be strong to survive." He laughed. Kyleigh looked at him, "Did you cut his finger?"

Trevor talked with Lonestar, "We have no idea where Jung's men are and which way they will come from. They may not since they know Michelle is not here. I hope she is far far away and safe. This with Bruce is very different."

"I am going to scout around town and see what's what. You say they have targeted Bruce now?" Lonestar said.

"I'll have a head to head with him. This may not take long and then again Jung's the boss, and he may drag it out. He has nothing else to do, but time in that prison to move his little pawns around."

Bruce, Unitus, and Roscoe had joined. "Where's Guy?"

Roscoe said, "He's busy as usual. I'll tell him all when I see him. I got a bone to pick with him anyways," holding up his finger.

"Lonestar … we appreciate you coming back, if anyone can flushed them out, I know you can do it. THE HOTEL had some unsavory characters and we got them. That might be a good place to start and at THE CASINO, also!" Trevor continued.

"The boys can get a roster of the guests, and the FBI can scan the guest photos. You can look and see if you recognize anyone in Jung's outfit. Bruce and Unitus can also check the profiles for any looking familiar to them. Just a thought!"

"That is a good idea. They usually travel in twos, and if they are Jung's men, they'll have drugs stowed somewhere in or outside the hotel."

Unitus said, "I can get an undercover cop with sunglasses to walk the dog around the cars at both places. Dressing the dog with a 'See N Eye' logo. Once a vehicle is identified. The tags can be matched to the room number. I've used this once before, and it also saved a lot of time. Bruce?"

"I was mainstream in Jung's organization and I know the higher ups. But if you can get a run on all the guests as you say, I'll take a look at the compiled photos. Jana can view them also. She was CIA and on Banks' payroll. She traveled with him on occasion to conduct business deals. She could have come in contact with a different clientele than I and Unitus. The network has a mass of underground operatives."

Trevor said, "We can use everyone's help so anyone else you want to call in, now is the time. Goodnight to all!"

They agreed to meet after breakfast to dig their heels in.

Lonestar finally had accepted Trevor's invitation to stay at Southfork. He had never stayed, but felt a need to be around family this time. He had become very fond of Trevor's dog Blackie and sat rubbing his head.

Lonestar sat by the fireplace staring at the logs. He hated it about Haruto. The last visit he had stayed at the Best Western motel, and they had become friends and he respected Haruto.

He recalled Haruto's wife, and her sister. He must ask Bruce to ask Jana, how they are doing?

Lonestar 's boys were their age and now they were off making lives for themselves, Littlefoot and Tenderfoot. Nicknames his wife had chosen.

This about Haruto's death had made him miss his wife. Her death still after all these years, made his heart ache.

CHAPTER THREE

Jason and Cheri were not seen at all for the first week, except leaving for school and suppertime. They were smiling and adjusting to married life. They just could not stop smiling at each other. In a crowd, it was like no one else mattered.

Corey told him, "You need to let her breath on her own for a minute or two!" Ellen elbowed him as they walked to their own room.

"Leave him be and take lessons from him," Ellen said.

Corey looked at his wife. "You did not say that. I'll see what I can do about that," he put three fingers in the air for her to see! Then he pointed at himself, and then at her.

"Sounds good to me! Bring it on," and she laughed knowing after working and night classes, he was exhausted. He would have only energy for one time a day for her. That was fine, but he was teasing Jason mercilessly.

She remembered their first month and asked him, "Honey you do remember not being able to keep your hands off me that first month? Now I have to remind you that I am here. Do you think the honeymoon is over?" and Ellen laughed.

"I'd say in four years probably. I've worn it out," Corey had REALLY messed up.

"How romantic. Don't come near me!" and Ellen slammed the bathroom door.

Corey ran to the door, "Open up! I didn't mean it like that."

"What did you mean it like?" she shouted.

"Open the door and I 'll show you. I love you! Every little thing about you! I hope to give you what you need for the next forty to fifty years. Just I am an old man now at twenty two. I have wore myself out loving you," he stated as fact.

Ellen flung open the door. "Okay, old man let me see what you got for me! Okay that 's looking good. Okay that is even better. Oh Corey honey. How I love makeup sex," Ellen was enjoying herself and so was Corey.

She was right! He had of late had his priorities wrong. It was not going to happen again. This wife of his was doing amazing things with her amazing body that was all for him. He may make it twice tonight, but three times, no way.

She said, "I know what you are thinking Corey, and yes way Let me show you!" and smiled sweetly at her old man. "I don't read Cosmo for nothing!"

"You are saying you get these ideas from a magazine?" he asked dumbfounded.

"Yes, guilty as charged!" she said as she made him jump to the ceiling, and she was laughing hysterically.

"Well I 'd said that feather didn't work well. You can relax honey, I won't try that ever again!"

"Let's talk for awhile," she said.

"Okay you talk all you want to, and I' ll listen to all before I go to sleep," one minute and he was snoring. She was talking away about this and that non-stop.

When she realized he was snoring, she kissed his cheek and smiled.

"I've done wore him out!" Ellen sat reading her magazine.

Janice was rubbing her belly where the baby was kicking, and she went for Adam to feel. He began kissing her stomach and rubbing "him".

The doctor had confirmed, it is a boy!

"He is going to be a football kicker for a major league team. I predict it. Wow! That was a good one. Sit back and give him room or sit on me, and let me rub him."

Adam was so in love with his wife, and the thought that they had passed the crucial month that most miscarriages happened. It sunk in that this was what real happiness was, multiplied my ten.

"You know how much I love you Janice, but I just have to say it again. I love you! Have you thought of a name?" Adam asked.

"Maybe Claiborne and call him Clay, or Joshua and call him Josh. What names have you been thinking of Babe?"

"Babe sounds good," he said with a chuckle and she hit him with a pillow.

"For real?" and Janice stretched on the sofa. Laying her head in his lap looking up at him.

"Okay, Andrew and call him Andy," he said softly.

"That's it! It is perfect Andy, Adam's son. My baby is going to have an awesome father. His mother is so proud to be Adam Joshua Shackleford 's wife.

"I think we need to celebrate with some sparkling ginger ale." The champagne glasses came out and they toasted to the baby's name.

"I think we need to seal the deal," he said and they did.

Madeline, Jana and Debbie were fixing breakfast for all. It was so much fun having a house full. Kyleigh and Beatrice were rounding up the kids, and the men were in the den.

Adriana and the kids were in the game room playing where the rocking horse, and mini trampoline were situated.

All hated to see Debbie have to go to work, but Marcus had sent his men over to pick her up. Tate rode with them, she was going nowhere without him. He'd hang around the slots until she was ready to leave, and they would call for the troops to come and escort them home.

This was going to be their daily routine. All was fine until that lumberjack came waltzing in and demanding a steak which they did not serve this night.

"I want to see the Chef!" he shouted.

Debbie heard and walked around the corner.

"Hot damn, you can't be the Chef?" his eyes were glassy as if he was on something. Debbie knew that look.

"What seems to be the problem?" She had her arms folded in defense mode.

"I want a medium rare steak to go along with a juicy KISS from you," he said.

She clicked her fingers and said, "Get him out of here!" and walked off while security wrestled with him and got him out of the casino.

Debbie was smiling until she saw Tate 's face. He was livid.

"He could have hurt you! What in the world was I thinking letting you work here. Turn in your notice!"

"You have got to be kidding!" she was so embarrassed in front of her kitchen crew.

She walked immediately into the bathroom where he could not come. He was right this man was mean, but it felt good for her to be able to stand up for herself, and have him tossed out was DOUBLY rewarding.

Tate just loves me so much. He does not want to see me hurt ever again. She was standing discussing this with herself.

In he walks as if they are at home, and the ladies were running out of the bathroom.

Tate said nothing but, "I'm sorry!" and held her.

Debbie said, "I'm sorry too. I know it frightened you, but I have to learn to fight back. I love my job! I will quit, if that is what you want me to do."

"We will talk about it at home. Okay? Can we leave the bathroom before the women have me tossed out, too!"

"Of course, can you call James please," she said as she walked to the kitchen to talk to her crew. She told her apprentice what she wanted done tomorrow because she was taking the rest of the day off.

Kirk Matterhorn was standing outside in the dark, watching as she and Tate got into the white limo. He had had too much coke, and his nerves were frazzled.

"I'll get you Miss High and Mighty. Just wait and see. May not be today or tomorrow, but I will fix you good!" he promised with a sneer.

He went around back and made his delivery to Frank, the blackjack dealer. The guards were watching him and reported the drop off to Marcus.

Marcus was angry, but held it in until he spoke to Trevor.

"Bingo boys! Seems there has been drug activity at THE CASINO. We must get the others, this is not a one man operation," Trevor stated.

They all agreed.

"If we get the little guy, maybe he will squeal on the others. If it's Jung's offshoots, these hicks will squeal to save their own carcasses," Roscoe needed to point this fact out.

Trevor got with the agents and they would hash it out, and come up with a short term and long term plan. They all needed to be on the same page.

Lonestar was just standing back observing and gave no advice. His method would be entirely different from theirs. No one asked, so he had learned a long time ago to lay low and assess the situation for himself.

When their plan didn't work, that's when he would step in. Trevor was his friend and no one was going to mess with this family. They had treated him like a family member, and he had always protected his family.

Trevor saw the look in Lonestar's eyes and knew what he was thinking, and he nodded. Yes was what the nod meant, you have my permission and blessing. No spoken word was needed.

Trevor continued talking to the boys and the agents, when IN came Tate and Debbie like a tornado.

Tate was clinching his jaw, and she said nothing to anyone which was totally unusual for Debbie. She was always happy when she got home. She would give an account of her day's events. Not tonight!

Madeline asked Tate, "What is wrong? Talk to me! You are too upset to talk to Debbie. Calm down, please! Let's take a walk. OK?" he was furious, but he agreed.

"You are right. She has been through enough, but you have to make her see that that job is not worth it! This lumberjack was hitting on my wife, and she had him thrown out. Do you think he is not going to come back and get even. SURE HE IS! I may not be there next time. Help me convince her that she needs to be home for right now with all else that's going on!"

Tate had finally wound down. Madeline knew to not say anything until he had it all out.

"I am glad you told me, and I do agree with you. Usually I take the female's side, but this time you are right, Tate. If you talk to her, she will resent it. You two will be at each other 's throat. So tell her I need to talk to her, and I will let her talk it out as you and I have done. Okay?" He nodded.

When he entered the bedroom she was nowhere in sight. He found her on the bathroom floor just sitting and staring. "I cannot do it. You are right. I am a weakling."

He held her and said nothing, "Madeline wants to talk to you when you feel like it."

"Maybe tomorrow I told them that I would not be at work tomorrow," and she dressed and went to bed.

He did also and just held her until they both fell asleep.

CHAPTER FOUR

Adriana was so glad when Unitus finally came to bed. He had showered and had her favorite Armani cologne on. It always reminded her of their first night at the gym.

He slid in beside her and she wrapped her arms around him. "So what is the verdict counselor?"

"I might get to take my wife on a spin around the world," he said and kissed her deeply.

"Won't work. Tell me what you guys have found out, and please tell me you are not getting involved and that Bruce is not either. Right?" she rubbed her leg between his.

"I may have to … if someone threatens my wife and kids' safety. Until then, I will give the so-called agents a chance. Don't you worry your pretty little head about that right now. You have better things to think about."

"And you are changing the subject. That is not a good sign. Fess up partner." She was not going to cave in just because he was rubbing every sensual spot that she had.

"They are going to set up a plan and I will let you know what they decide. There!" He was not going to let her get away with bossing him around tonight because they were not at home. She had to be quiet.

"Our dog and all the others are outside. If you holler, they will eat your hubby alive! So kiss me quick and open wide."

"Oh my, Unitus" she said and he kissed her softly. "You really have missed me today!" he sealed her lips more firmly.

Marcus met with Trevor and stated, "I am not having this going on at my business. I'll have my men take them out." He was wanting some answers.

Trevor said, "I know, but we want to do this right and take them ALL out at once. The message we will send is to stay away from this area for good. We are monitoring them. When the time comes I will give you a call. But until then, just trust us and our families can celebrate together."

Marcus shook Trevor's hand. "The one thing that really concerned me badly is this incident with Debbie."

"What incident with Debbie?" Marcus's brows furrowed.

"I thought you should know that guy we are watching that dropped off to your dealer, made a pass at her and she had him ousted. They say he stated he would be BACK, and when he does we will get him. If you could talk to her and ask her to take a mini vacation, I would appreciate it," he paused.

"She doesn't want to let you down. Madeline has finally got her to talk. If you don't say where you heard it that would be a good thing," Trevor frowned.

Marcus paced and said, "They told me this happened in the buffet area, but they failed to tell me it was Debbie. Tate is angry, I am sure. I'll talk to her tomorrow. She is too sweet a girl to work in the casino anyway. Maybe we can work something else out. Definitely she should not be there while this other mess is going on. I do agree whole heartily."

Madeline had listened to Debbie.

Debbie told her that Tate meant more to her than that job.

"I'm not going back. I will talk to Mr. Buchanan tomorrow," and she smiled at Madeline.

"I am so glad to see that smile back on your face young lady," Madeline gave her a hug.

"Me, too!" Tate came strolling in as if he had not heard what she said. He hugged her and Madeline.

"Thank you!" Tate said.

The others were coming to life and the kids were hollering, "I'm hungry!"

Debbie looked at Tate and said, "My services are needed after all. Would you like to help me in the kitchen?"

"No what I would like," and he whispered in her ear.

"Since that is not going to happen, I would be glad to help you!" and Tate grinned.

Debbie said, "I am glad to see that smile back on your face!"

The women kind of let those two cook by themselves this morning, and Madeline sat back and played with the grand kids, and chatted with the daughter-in-laws.

"Geez I have miss you 'all. This house was so empty when everyone left last time. Let's not forget to set a place for Michelle and Robert until they return. I will be glad when we hear from them. It was between six months and a year last time." That was the most Madeline had said in awhile.

They all gave her a hug even the little ones ran to GM.

She had them calling her GM instead of Grandma.

"Gotta train them when they are little like I did Guy and Roscoe!"

Jasmine and John Wayne were becoming real country bumpkins. They had started making vegetable boxes in the little greenhouse that they had made.

They purchased hay for the winter and had filled the loft. Their pantry... they were stocking slowly. When the snows come, Robert would have all the wood split for the fireplace.

Michelle would slip and say his real name and vice versa.

"It's a good thing we don't live in town," she said.

"Why hon?" he grinned. "Because you like to scream my name?"

"Truly I would call you day or night my beloved by the wrong name. You only have one to remember. I have three to answer to. Hmm!" John continued.

Jasmine strutted to the sink and started peeling potatoes. She was wearing those high heel boots like she did in the big city and her hair piled on top of her head. The better he could kiss her neck, and that off one shoulder sweater that with one small tug would expose a bare breast. She did not like to wear undergarments of any kind unless they were in the city.

"Such a waste! Women pay all that money for lacy stuff and men just rip it off. Doesn't make sense," she would always tease him saying it and looking into his eyes.

"If I wear it, it will be to sleep in and nothing else. Oops I don't like to sleep in anything. Right darling?"

"You are so right! Such a waste! Sleeping in the raw works best for me, too! Don't you change that habit just because it gets cold here at night. I got enough heat to keep us both warm. Raven, Michelle or Jasmine, do you hear me?"

"Wonder which one will show up tonight to be with my husband. Will it be Raven, Michelle, or Jasmine?" she continued and batted her eyelashes at him.

"The new John Wayne will step up to all three. Just bring them all!" Robert's eyes were ogling her.

"When we ever get back to civilization you will not know how to act! Lusting after three women at one time. You better be glad all three are ME, or you would be in big big trouble Mister!" wielding that kitchen knife at him to emphasize what would happen to him, if he strayed.

He grabbed her and wrestled the knife away just because she let him.

"You are all the woman I will ever need, and I am needing you now!"

"My dear John! Do you want to eat today?" she asked.

He nodded his head and said, "Boy, do I ever!"

"Just a few chosen words from you and that's all I want to do. Gobble you up! How do you do that?" he asked and stared at her with squinted eyes.

"What peel potatoes?" she said licking her lips then sucking on her bottom lip. She got her switchblade out of her jeans.

"Come I will give you a lesson," she dared him.

He came toward her again and she threw the switchblade precisely and it stuck into the wall with one fluid motion.

"So not to endanger you nor I. I thought it best, I get rid of that!" she said softly with that come hither look.

He scooped her up and she was kicking which only excited him more. She knew she'd let him win, it would be worth it.

Bruce was getting flack from Jana and she was right. He had spent years trying to nail Jung.

"I can do whatever you need to be done, and you know it. I don't have a bounty on my head. One screw up and Adriana may NOT be able to get you out this time!" She was spitting fire. Pacing and talking in Japanese which he understood clearly, and it was not lovey-dovey words either.

That's why he loved her. She was so passionate about everything. He would try to stay out of it, but he made no promises.

Adriana had had that same conversation with Unitus. He had made no promises either. "A man with two children should know better. You are the town's DA now, did you forget! You wanted me to stay home for six month's. Yeah!" she walked off.

Bruce and Unitus sat at the kitchen table drinking coffee. "You got the third degree talk, too!"

"Yeah, comes with the territory! Isn't like when we were single! Those were the days!" and they clinked their coffee cups.

"Not a soul, gave a damn about me. Not even my mother!Now she kisses my cheek after Jana does!" Bruce said.

"Not a soul gave a damn about me, except you Bruce. Now I got Adriana and the kids and my new job!" Unitus sighed.

"I can't mess this up with Jana!"

"I can't mess this up with Adriana!"

"We are so hen-pecked."

"Yep, I'm out!" Unitus declared.

Bruce said, "Me, too!"

Agent Sterling was in with Trevor. "We had the Matterson lumberjack followed. He is getting his stash at the country store called 'Floyd's'. I've got a stakeout there. In the past three weeks a semi has stopped and made two deliveries. That store is not big enough and has nothing much in it, to get deliveries that often," he paused and paced.

"We looked deeper and under further review found the truck driver. His name is Ferguson. We think he is the link to the drugs that Matterson had. We are going to tail him and see where he gets his merchandise. Then I will assign NARCs to the loading docks wherever and follow this operation till we get them all. That's where we stand at the moment."

"That is a good plan and it is going to take time, I know. We are behind you, if you need help just ask. Lonestar is chomping at the bit."

"There is one other thing that has been strange. A principal of one of the small private schools on the mountain above Floyd's has been picking up drugs. My man said he is getting sloppy and setting up with the wealthy people in his area. He was heard saying that he supplies their parties "with fun stuff.""

"He asked my lady undercover agent, if she wanted some fun stuff." Sterling said.

Bruce and Jana had walked by and over hear that last bit.

Bruce asked, "What is the man's name? Glen Robertson?"

"As a matter-of-fact it is, do you know him?" Sterling asked.

"I applied for a teacher's position at his school. Jana and I stopped by that store Floyd's to get …... a drink. He turned me down said, I was overqualified. Never would have pegged him for a seller. If you need me and Jana to ride through anytime, let me know. I really like that school. Hate to see it be run by that type of fellow," Bruce was talking himself into another tongue lashing.

Jana said, "That is something, we prefer not to do gentlemen. You all are doing a fine job! Honey we have to go. Madison is waiting for his GRANDFATHER to play with him," she put her arm in his, and maneuvered him out the door of Trevor's den.

She let his hand go, and pranced in front of him with that pencil skirt that had a three inch slit up the back. Those three inch heels that she always wore, and she was definitely proving a point. She had his attention as if saying "You want to leave all this" without saying a word.

He said, "You are right Jana. They are doing a marvelous job!" He was back pedaling big time.

"You are so going to get it tonight! Just when I thought we were on the same page, you pull this!" Jana was patting her foot and had crossed her arms. That was not a good sign.

Bruce poured her a cup of hot tea and himself some strong coffee. Sitting down beside her saying, "I apologize, but I did include you, and I did not say anything behind your back."

She sipped her tea and said, "That is true! That is an improvement. You including me may make your bed softer!"

CHAPTER FIVE

THE CASINO was rocking tonight. They had a special guest performing. The Embers were there to play beach music and the bar was hopping. The gamblers were spending big bucks, and the slots were ding ding dinging.

Roscoe had put extra security on tonight, usually there would be some rowdy people that would have to be escorted out on any given Saturday night.

The parking lots were being monitored, and the black jack dealer Travis, continued to be under surveillance. Kirk and he had made contact, and the boys moved in, and arrested both. They had kept it outside last time, but this time had brought it indoors. The agents seized all the evidence of the drug transaction. The camera video tape would also be evidence.

The main goal tonight was to interrogate Kirk and make him squeal stated Sterling. If he wants to work with us in nabbing Ferguson, we may can get his sentence reduced.

"Man you are crazy! If I do any time, they will kill me in prison. I have to have a better deal than that!" Kirk was not thinking clearly.

"Well sonny boy. I just taped that, so while you are detoxing reconsider my offer. You will NOT get it again!" Lt. Coltrane knew Kirk well. He had been in and out of jail numerous times usually for fighting, but this was serious.

Coltrane knew he could not use the tape, but Kirk didn't know that. The interrogation continued, Sterling was pleased.

Kirk had given the exact time for his pick up at Floyd's. Floyd had told him once in the past when Ferguson would arrive. "Just like clockwork Ferguson is always on schedule! You be here Kirk when I tell you to ... do ya hear?" Floyd would say to his nephew.

The Peterbilt truck was rolling down the mountain and had just left Charlotte's Railway where he had picked up a delivery. The agents were in place and saw with whom Ferguson was talking. A large black man by the name of Tito and his two bodyguards met Ferguson. They took two satchels from the trunk of the black Cadillac Escalade.

Ferguson gave him a briefcase probably money from the last collection of selling of the goods. Tito flipped through it and shook his hand. Tito held it and squeezed Ferguson's hand until he was almost on the ground. It was to emphasize that he had better do as told, and not be a penny short.

Ferguson straightened, and kept nodding his head to every thing that Tito was saying, letting him know he understood.

Then he got in his truck and drove off. The deal had been recorded with high powered lens. The agents went about their regular jobs on the railway. They had infiltrated the area, but good.

The key was the railway system went all the way to Miami. Someone on that train was supplying Tito. It was all coming together. Jung was sending it by ship, the train was unloaded, and then deliveries were being made throughout the USA by truck. It was going to take a lot of manpower for this raid.

Trevor talked to Madeline and said he never imagined this little hick store would uncover this mass of information for the DEA. Jung's men are going to be so busy pretty soon that they won't even be looking our way.

She smiled at him. "I hope so. I surely hope so."

Bruce and Unitus, Guy and Roscoe, Tate and Adam all got together to celebrate the news. "Guess we can all can go home then!"

Trevor said, "Nothing has happened to warrant that. This is just the preliminary stage. So cool your jets until I get word!"

Marcus was filled in about the Kirk incident and Trevor informed him of the plans. "We are still not out of the woods yet, but it is looking better."

Lonestar walked up, "There are THREE new men at the Best Western just arrived this morning. I went by to speak to the lady that fixes breakfast there. She always gives me a free cup of coffee, and I asked if she had seen any strange characters lately?" he paused to look at Trevor.

"That's when I spotted them. They had large duffle bags and the kind I use to carry my rifle in when I broke it down. They are either here for a gun convention or they mean for someone to die. Just a thought that the family should stay PUT for the time being."

Trevor shook his hand.

"Thanks friend, "Trevor looked at the ceiling.

The agents were busy getting the information on these guys and the male family members were agreeable to remain, and the women would be told later.

When Adam got home he talked with Marcus and he said, "I just can't imagine what that family is going through again."

Adam stayed with Janice for the next week. "She does not need you in a line of fire and upsetting that baby with one month to go!" he hugged Eunice.

"Jason, you and Cheri …. Corey, you and Ellen all bunker down. I love all of you as Trevor loves his family. Everyone in one spot makes sense. The guards are doubled here. So our fortress is secure. No one needs to worry. If anything looks suspicious come and tell me."

Everyone agreed with Marcus.

At the table Jason said to his wife, "You are in the family that takes care of its own. Now give me a smile."

Cheri's smile was bright as sunshine and she whispered in his ear, "I love you!" He could barely eat. She was making circles with her index finger on his leg. With the long tablecloth, no one else could see.

"If you don't stop, I will have to sit here all night. You will have to go upstairs by yourself," then Jason grinned and grabbed her hand.

"You wouldn't dare!" Cheri countered.

"No, I wouldn't," he said and they held hands under the table.

Eunice looked at Marcus, "Does anyone want to talk about their day?" she liked to hear things about their day.

Each shared something about their day. Marcus did not share a drug transaction had occurred at his casino, and now this at Trevor and Madeline's.

"Janice have you and Adam got a nursery in mind, only one month to go?"

"No, I have been waiting to shop with Adam and he has been working so hard," she said and patted his leg and missed.

He immediately sat straight up, "We have to ask! If we can use the next bedroom? I would like to take the adjoining door off, to have a way to get to the baby's room. We didn't want to do anything without asking first."

Marcus said, "Of course. That will be perfectly alright! You can even shop online. Eunice didn't Madeline teach you how? Show Janice and let's have this week to decorate it, just like you two want it."

Adam was happy with that he wouldn't have liked to be dragged around from store to store. He smiled.

Ellen and Cheri chimed in that they would love to help, while the guys shook their heads yes.

"Yes you girls help yourselves. It's on me!" Marcus said and was smiling brightly at Eunice. His life was so full now. He could not imagine a day without her and the family.

The days that followed were filled with laughter and excitement. Adam had the door off, and the boys had helped him move the other bed and door, to the basement for storage.

The nursery was done in blues, and the crib was matched to the dresser and bureau, a beautiful cherry. They found a changing pad the color of the baby linens, and put it on the dresser which made it a perfect changing table. The glider- rocker was delivered with the crib. The mini sofa, they had decided to keep it, so both could play with the baby on it.

The navy blue and blue plaid bedding was so elegant.

Adam said, "I think I could just lay on this floor and sleep for a week."

Janice quickly said, "That is our bedroom," pointing to the plush bed in the next room that awaited. "The baby needs you to rub his head," she said then blushed.

"It is done. Do you like it?" Janice asked him.

"If you like it, I love it! But I have to rub the baby's head tonight. I have been missing my little one," and she sat in his lap and he rubbed and rubbed.

"That is not the baby's head, dear," she was leaning further back and he had her in a reclining position.

"You always know where it feels the best. Let me see if I can rub our baby's head another way," she slid onto him and he was not complaining. It had been a week.

Her car wreck injuries and pelvis had been strained from the body's weight. At this moment, she was really loving his advances and no thought of pain, only need.

He was going slow. Then she said, "You got to do it right."

He took a deep breath, "I can't I might hurt you."

She grabbed his shoulders. He was panting.

"Baby you are so sexy when you take control!"

Guy asked Kyleigh, "How are you and Beatrice doing?" He paused and her eyes stared at him.

He never paused unless he was trying to find the words to tell her something important.

"I know as best friends, this is a time you and she plan a lot of things. Don't plan anything for another month!"

Kyleigh came to him, "What do you mean? That we can't go home for another month? What is going on? Tell me?" she beat on his chest.

"I can only say that you are safe here. Madison is safe here.

I will be with you all the time that I am not working. I know you are angry, and it is okay. I am angry, too."

He was gritting his teeth as he held her. The same men that had helped kidnapped his wife, may still be out there and she knew it. It terrified her and he could do nothing to reassure her, except tell her that he would be here THIS time to protect her. Though Banks was dead, the rest had connections with Jung. Jung had been Banks 's boss.

She finally let him go when Madison came running in all excited about the play day.

"We are going to the ball field and play some baseball, Mommy!" he said with enthusiasm.

Guy said to her, "I need to talk to Roscoe."

"Roscoe, Brother of mine you have forgotten something?" Guy said angrily stating a fact.

"What's got you all in a huff?" Roscoe standing in front of him, nose to nose.

"You have!" and he didn't move a muscle.

"Me? Me? Moi? What in the daylights are you talking about Guy?" Roscoe growled at him.

"You haven't told Beatrice! Kyleigh is devastated and Madison thinks he is going to a ball field!" Guy shouted.

"Haven't told me what Roscoe?" Beatrice asked as she was folding the kids 's clothing from the laundry basket.

"Holy crap! Guy give me a break! She was doing the laundry!" Roscoe was pacing now.

"Well you two do everything else in the laundry room so why don't you tell her in there!" and Guy walked off.

"Low blow, Brother! Low blow!" Roscoe shouted.

"Beatrice can you step into my office," and he escorted her to the laundry room. Where he told her the situation, and asked her to please … please … smooth it over with Kyleigh and Madison for his sake.

"No sex?" Beatrice pointed to the table.

"Not this time. I wish but brother has slam dunked my libido in the laundry door moments ago. It probably is traumatized and will never work in here again!" he grimaced.

Beatrice kissed him and walked closer to him.

"It will work anywhere else … have no fear, but not in here!" Roscoe reassured her.

Beatrice found Kyleigh and they talked, and the kids played, and all were fine with not going to the field today.

Beatrice said, "Besides we have more time to plan, plan, and plan some more!" they both were beaming.

Kyleigh was smiling when Guy and Roscoe checked in on them.

They high-fived in the hallway.

"Your strategy worked!" Guy said to Roscoe.

Tate said, "Honey I am so thankful you are home and were not in that mess at the casino. The man that hit on you is in jail for now, but a lot of other stuff is going on. Guy, Roscoe and I are helping Trevor with this!"

Debbie looked at him. "If you get yourself killed, what am I supposed to do? HUH ? Yeah ! Never thought of that had you! Not going to happen, buddy. If I got to bunker down, so are you!"

She grabbed him by the collar and kissed him big time. This once shy girl was now taking charge.

"Wow!" he managed to say. She was looking into his soul.

"No one is going to get killed ... but you can keep during that if you want to!" Tate said with her between his legs.

Bruce came by and said, "Get a room!" smiling back at Jana so Tate couldn't see. Jana winked at Debbie.

"Good idea!" Tate said and picked Debbie up and shoved the door open to their room, then locked it.

Later he said, "I'll tell Trevor he has to count me out. I have to stay with the woman ... I mean women and children to protect you 'all," and gave her a smile. She smiled back and stretched lazily in the bed with a sheet covering most of her.

"Do you really have to do it now?" she wanted him to remember this day as a day that she was worth his time and effort. She patted the bed, even though he had fully dressed. He seemed to be stripping his clothes off much faster. His wife had just shown him how good it could be in the middle of the afternoon.

He would be a fool, if he didn't jump back in THAT bed!

PART TWENTY ONE

CHAPTER ONE

It had been six months, and Jasmine and John Wayne were driving 300 miles away from their present home and calling home on a disposable phone.

"Madeline! It is me Jasmine and my husband John. We called to say all is well!" she was teary eyed.

"Oh honey and I am so thankful you call. We love you! Be safe and too much has happened, stay clear. Kiss John for me and call another time, honey. I'll explain later," GM hung up.

Jasmine stared at the phone, and John took it and stomped it to pieces. Throwing it into the trash dumpster before he took his "violet" eyed beauty into his arms.

"Something is happening bad at home ... she told me to stay away. It is not good. MY gut says go, but she wants us to not get hurt that would kill her to think that I reacted to something she said."

His gray eyes bore a hole into her psyche. "You are my wife and I want you to remember we are a team. If we leave, we leave together. Do you hear me? You will not do anything without me. Promise?" John knew that look. "You are not back home, this is different country. I am use to country.

I was raised on an English farm. That is why I fell right in with the chores. The city was not my life, I just adjusted to gain a name for myself. I thought that would make me happy. Fame, did not. Only you have made me happy," John admitted.

"We will stay and I will call in three months. If this is where you want to settle for now, but Hendersonville is my home that I hope we can live out our old age there!" Jasmine smiled at him as they got in the old truck, and headed back to the rented farm house. There was no way they could trace that call and they were safe.

They stopped by the pound and adopted a dog. He was half hound dog. Someone had abandoned him. Due to his age no one wanted him. His name was Clancy and he fell in love with Jasmine. He sat in the back seat of the truck's cab.

They fed the horses and three new baby chicks and oriented Clancy to everything.

They brought him inside for the night so he would not run off. He plopped right between them. John looked at Jasmine and said, "Houston we have a problem!"

"Just for tonight so he will know he is loved. Please!" she begged and he smiled.

"One night only! Good night you two," and he turned the light off.

She could feel him rubbing the dog instead of her.

"She said, "You are so right! ONLY one night. Clancy is getting my caresses and I am super jealous," and she giggled.

"He has got to have his own bed," John said.

The next night, he howled and howled until they let him in. He had a bed made by the fireplace on the floor, but up the steps he had gone and got in their bed.

"What on earth are we going to do?" she asked.

"Just like me. It only took one time in your bed and I kept coming back!" he smiled a devilish grin.

"Why don't we sleep down here tonight and maybe he will sleep down here tomorrow night!" he suggested.

"Then we can run up the steps and lock the door," she was in love with the man, but the dog was working his way into her heart with that sad face. She had always wanted a dog, but never could afford to feed one.

"Oh no!" she shouted.

"What are you talking about?" he was concerned.

"I forgot to get him dog food. He is going to starve!" She was frantic.

He grabbed her. The dog growled. "Well fellow I was going to tell her you eat scrapes from the table, and if you don't like them. It is because she likes vegetables! I like meat so we will see whose side of the table you sit at by tonight!"

He removed his hand from her buttocks very carefully.

"Wonder if he can climb ladders?" John grinned at her.

"I think we will have to test the waters tomorrow. I sure am horny," Jasmine teased.

He walked over and put her across his shoulder like a caveman, and walked up the stairs. He told the dog to sit and he sat.

He took her into the bathroom and locked the door.

The dog did not move from his spot.

He was doing amazing things and she was not screaming as usual, and he was worried she was not happy.

She looked at him when he asked what was wrong, "I can't holler the dog will go crazy!"

"If you don't holler, I am going to go crazy!" he stated.

"OK, just bring it on!" and he did.

She said, "I was afraid if I hollered, you'd stop!" She laughed, and held up two fingers. Twice he had satisfied her, but who was keeping score.

As they showered she asked, "How did you get dear old Clancy to sit?"

"I gave him a piece of meat. All day every time he sat," he said. "That is training."

"So you have been training me, too! Every time I bark you give me a piece of meat and I sleep all night!"

"No ... it is you that has trained me to beg for my supper. When you feed me, you feed me good. I come to be fed every night, and like to be petted and have my head rubbed."

She rubbed his head, and he said, "Not that head!"

"I know, but worth a try," she was drying him and kissing him, and he was holding up three fingers.

She rose and licked each of his fingers separate. He could not believe that her just sucking on his fingers could cause such an erection, and all she could do was smile and raise three fingers.

She used her index finger to reel him in to her. She was holding onto the sink for dear life, and he pulled her back and forward. It only got better.

She threw her head back and HOLLERED.

Later, "Clancy did you hear?" John asked and smiled.

"Michelle phoned. Her name is now Jasmine and Robert's name is John. They are fine, Trev. I don't know their last name nor do I know where they are living. I told her not to come home!" Madeline was weeping as Trevor held her.

"It won't be long before she can come home. Robert will take care of her. We will see her within this coming year. When we do they can have body guards around the clock, I will see to it. Don't cry!"

Trevor could not stand to see Madeline cry.

"Trev these are happy tears. They are ALIVE! Everything else is trivial. Now tell me what we can do?" Madeline did not want to be left out.

"We are leaving everything up to the SBI and FBI … and Lonestar. Roscoe's men are still providing security, and they are checking the houses daily. That's it in a nutshell!"

"So none of my boys are involved. Bruce, Roscoe, Guy, nor Tate? I will hold you to it Trevor!" Madeline meant it.

The kids were making a fort in the game room. Roscoe had a tepee delivered, so they could put that together also. Then they could watch old cowboy movies with the little ones.

Roscoe said to Guy, "That's the only way they will learn how to play Cowboys and Indians. Like we did when we were little."

"Yeah! Do you remember went I tied you to the clothesline and dirt clogged you?" Guy asked.

"Yeah I remember," Roscoe grinned. "It was worth it! You could not sit down for a week and no ice cream. I had all the ice cream I wanted that week. That is a FOND memory."

Roscoe was gloating.

Guy was frowning, "Yeah you won that one, but if I had burned you at the stake? You are a lucky man!"

"But then you went and sneaked me a cup of the best chocolate Rocky Road ice cream into my room and I FORGAVE you," Roscoe smiled.

"What you mean you forgave me! I was the one with big bruises from the dirt clogs," Guy huffed.

They were standing toe to toe and Madeline walked in.

"Boys! Boys! Not that again. You two that happened almost twenty years ago. Let it go!" Madeline refereed then and now.

"Those were the good old days," they grinned at each other.

They hugged Madeline and she was happy that they had survived those battles when they were little.

"Now help these children build these memories and secure the structures so they won't hurt themselves," and she left to play with Vanderbilt who was not a baby any more.

"Adriana that boy is getting to be a handful," Madeline said.

"Yes! Just like his daddy!" Adriana said loud enough so Unitus could hear, and he smiled and blew her a kiss.

"Angel is my petite little darling that takes after her mother!" Adriana was laying it on thick.

Unitus emerged, "Yes she is! Gets her way about every thing. I mean EVERYTHING!" and he walked off.

Adriana told Madeline, "He is right. I admit it. He gives me everything I want!"

Unitus froze mid-step, turned and smiled.

"You want to see him run?" Adriana said.

Madeline asked, "Whatever do you mean?"

Adriana had her figure back and she rose in her tight dress pants, and bend over to the floor without squatting to retrieve the truck Vanderbilt had thrown onto the floor, and turned with that come hither look at him.

Unitus flew to the bathroom.

Madeline said, "I'm going to try that one on Trevor. "Well low and behold here he is now. "Throw that toy honey, I got to test this out."

She bent over in her jeans and high heel cowboy boots and looked back at Trevor and licked her lips. He flew to the bedroom because the bathroom was occupied.

GM high- fived Adriana and said, "You have taught this old dog a new trick!" and they both laughed.

Beatrice and Kyleigh heard them laughing and so did Debbie who was in the kitchen, "I know I missed something good." The women shared and all day one or the other was trying out their new found trick.

Madeline said, "You know we must all be bored. We have to find something else to increase their mental capacity because we know everything else WORKS. That is our assignment for tonight!" and they all laughed.

The men heard them all laughing and said, "This is not good!" in unison.

The next morning the females all said, "They only have one track minds!" in unison. Laughter brought the men running.

The FBI had arrested Glen Robertson as he produced the cocaine to sell to the undercover agent. Then they waited for the truck to pull in, and he took something into Floyd's store. They arrested them. The dogs sniffed out the location in the store and in the truck. The truck was impounded.

The Department of Social Services was notified to help Floyd 's wife since there was no other close kin. She was taken to a Non Ambulatory Care Center.

The interrogation of these three took some time. Each thought the other was blabbing, so they all wanted to cut a deal. The Peterbilt truck was driven by an agent at the designated time that Ferguson said he was expected at the Rail-yard in Charlotte.

The black Escalade pulled in, and came to the truck. The agents opened fire since the bodyguards were pulling out semi automatic handguns. Tito did not move nor did he move his hands from the satchel. The satchel had the cocaine inside, and they needed it as evidence. He knew it. The negotiator was busy, and a police helicopter was circling overhead.

"Put your hands above your head," the megaphone was blasting.

He did, and they seized the bag. Tito being the only one alive was a good thing. "I know my rights. I have a lawyer."

"If you want a deal, waive the lawyer. We have all the ones you deal with, in custody. You know what we want and you can have a new name and identity. The man above you is who?"

"MARCUS BUCHANAN!" Tito said. It was recorded.

The agents were in shock. This had to be a joke. They had to proceed with the protocol and all procedures were followed properly. Tito had been told by Jung to say this, and it had worked. He could see it on their faces, and he laughed. They handcuffed him, and put him in the back of the police car.

Sterling didn't know how he was going to tell Trevor, but it had to be done, and done today.

Lonestar followed the three men that had come into town and they went straight to the Buchanans. Marcus must have hired more security.

He reported it to Trevor. As the FBI pulled up to the house, Trevor asked Lonestar to stay, and he did. Sterling knew the last time Marcus was at this house, and he appeared to be frightened. His men were on the way to arrest Mr. Buchanan.

He had to talk to Trevor, and Trevor said we can talk here. He had heard it on the scanner.

His insides were churning. Sterling reported exactly what went down. Trevor told him, "You have the wrong man!"

"If so, he will be proven innocent, but I have to do my job.

I am sorry!" Sterling turned and left.

"Lonestar will you get Unitus ... no one else."

Unitus came out and he knew whatever it was … it was colossal. Unitus was the DA. He had to prepare him for the backlash, and have him stabilize Adriana as best he could for the children 's sake.

Trevor told him, and he let out a Tarzan yell ... loud enough for Haruto to hear him in heaven.

CHAPTER TWO

Trevor said, "I have called James to drive to Marcus or wherever you need to go. Neither of you need to drive. We will take care of the kiddos. Don't worry about them. Just do what you can and I will be here, if you need me. Call me and let me know what's what. I will be working a few angles."

"Thanks Trevor. Just ask her to come outside and no one else please!" Unitus asked and Trevor hugged him.

Lonestar would never forget that holler Unitus made. It was the one that Haruto had told him about. "If the man on the mountain does a big Tarzan yell ... his family is in big trouble, and we Ninjas must help!" he had not forgot those words and he would help for Haruto's name sake.

Adriana came out smiling, and then she saw Unitus standing beside the white limo, and the door was open for her to get in. She had never seen this look on Unitus's face.

"Is someone dead? I have to know. Tell me!" she was shouting and then she became quiet.

"I am sorry. I wish I did not have to tell you this, but I have to quickly. So we can put our heads together, and try and FIX this!" He told her about the bust from start to finish and then he told her what the man named Tito said.

118

She screamed so loud, he was afraid she may have burst her heart. He held her as she cried, "It's a lie!" over and over.

"We have to prepare a case. I as the DA, will have to withdraw from this case. I cannot prosecute my father-in-law.

I do not know who will, but we have to be one step ahead of whoever it is. You as your father's lawyer have to be present to hear everything. They have asked him, and you will ask him or do you want me to do it?" Unitus paused.

"I pray he heard the Miranda rights, and didn't say anything. Are you okay now?" Unitus hugged her again. He called the police detective to see, if he was there.

They said, "Yes."

"James to the police station!" and he held Adriana tight and prayed she did not faint. "We will go as both his lawyers. They cannot deny his lawyers."

"I cannot go in there. I will wait for you here. PLEASE understand darling. Anyone … but him, I'd go right in there!"

"It's okay baby. Just lay down and rest. It may take awhile."

She laid down and cried. James handed her tissues through the connecting window. "If there is anything else you need just ask me, and I will get it!" James said.

Adriana said, "Thank you so much!" she blew her nose and wiped her eyes. She just rested like her wonderful husband asked her to do.

Marcus was in an orange jumpsuit, and he stood as Unitus came in. "This is my lawyer!" "Now you can ask me anything."

"We need to confer first before all your questions. That is his right," Unitus said. They left for them to talk.

"How is Adriana?" Marcus asked.

"We have to talk about you. You do not say a word, if I look at you. Is that clear. I have to know have you ever been involved with drugs in the past?" Unitus asked.

"Have you ever sold drugs?"

"When I was in my twenties I used them for recreational use after college. Not since then, I swear," he coughed and continued.

"Never. This is a holy nightmare! Anyone that knows me knows that. I have money, but I worked for it legally!" Marcus stated firmly as fact.

"I believe you. This person must have been instructed to implicate you. We have to prove it. Say nothing. Plead the fifth or say ask my lawyer," Unitus waved to the two-way mirror for them to come back.

They interrogated him for two hours with no questions answered. Unitus asked for him to be let out on his own recognizance. "I know the judge is in his chambers, may I go speak with him?"

The judge told Unitus as long as he appears in court as required. "Have him sign a written promise, and I will sign it only because it is you, Unitus."

"Judge I have to step aside, and let the assistant DA take my place. You understand I will be defending my father-in-law. Thank you sir." Marcus signed and redressed, and they left.

"Oh Daddy! I am so sorry. I know you did nothing wrong. This horrible person will pay for this. Unitus, you did good. I love you both." Adriana was just chattering away her nerves were getting the best of her.

Neither man said a word. "Is he out on bail?" she asked. Unitus shook his head.

"Own recognizance, dear," her father said. "I signed a little slip of paper. I hope I am around for it," and he coughed.

"What do you mean sir?" Unitus asked holding Adriana.

"I mean, if I don't have a heart attack. Lord knows what this has done to Eunice and the children. I will sue them for all they are worth," and he paled and continued to cough.

"Daddy please take this in stride. We will be there with you every step of the way," Adriana stated and Unitus nodded.

"Sir, do you need to go by the hospital and get your heart checked out? James drive us!" Unitus trying to cover all the bases.

"It would prove that this false accusation had caused you undue stress. We need to have it recorded," Unitus stated.

"Yes, son-in-law! I think that would be a very good idea and Eunice can come to the hospital to see me. I definitely am staying overnight for tests!" and winked at Adriana.

"My daddy has his MOJO back," Adriana kissed him on the cheek. "While you are with daddy, honey. I'll have James take me to get Eunice."

"Sounds good," and Unitus kissed her thoroughly.

"Hey! You two, I am a sick man," and he got in the wheelchair and Unitus pushed him in as James drove off.

"Are you hurting?" Unitus knew.

"Real bad, son hurry! I knew Adriana could not handle it!You are quick on your observation," Marcus said.

Unitus hit the floor running, "He's having a heart attack!"

The little policeman that Adriana had broke his hand the day she delivered Angel, was working tonight as extra security.

He said, "Let this man through, get the doctor quick or you 'all will be sorry! Mr. Universe means business!"

One of the nurses said," That is the billionaire that donated the children 's wing and named it after his granddaughter."

"Call all hands on deck. Now! Even the CEO of this hospital is to be here! He said if he ever comes to this hospital for anything … they are to be called immediately. Call them!" the head nurse shouted to her staff.

Unitus wheeled him in and the doctor was fast assessing and ordering tests, blood work, and blood type matching. Within thirty minutes, they were prepping him for surgery. His heart had stopped once, Unitus said to himself, "Thank God! Adriana was not here."

He called Trevor and asked if Madeline and he could come, and help him deal with Adriana and Eunice.

Unitus paced and prayed. The O.R. waiting room was quieter than the emergency room, so his nerves were calming. It was taking Adriana a long time to get back.

Madeline and Trevor came up to sit with him. Madeline hugged him as did Trevor. "I appreciate you both coming. It doesn't look good. I don't understand where Adriana is? I don't want to call her because she doesn't know he is in surgery. Do you think I should? He is hanging on."

He finally did call. "Adriana are you alright?"

"We are in the emergency room with all this excitement Janice is having the baby, and Eunice needed to help Adam. Come here and save me!" she was laughing hysterically.

"OK! On my way!" he told Madeline and Trevor what was happening. "I'll be right back!" then he turned "Madeline do you want to help Eunice and Adam while Trevor helps me and Adriana?"

"Yes and both you go. I'll be here!" Trevor waited and prayed for his friend Marcus.

Madeline got to Eunice and Adam, and hugged them and waited. Once they got Janice in the delivery room, Adam went back with her. She was in so much pain. He looked like he needed Trevor, but Unitus stepped up.

"You OK? Take it from me ... ask for orange juice it will help, if you have a long wait." he laughed. The tension was getting to him.

"I have to go be with Adriana. They are operating on Marcus that is why Madeline is here with Eunice. I am here if you need me, you have my cell number. I have to go for now. Trevor will be down in a few minutes, so you are not alone," Unitus left and held his wife up when he told her Marcus was in the Operating Room. Madeline and Eunice walked behind them.

They sat and waited. Taking turns going to sleep. Several recliners had been brought in for them. Six hours later the doctor came out.

"He is stabilized. The next 72 hours is crucial. His heart was pretty damaged and we fixed it." he paused. Then said, "He will be ICU for the next few days so you people need to get some rest and we will call, if there is any change."

Eunice said, "I need to stay." Madeline said she would stay with her. Trevor said he was going to check on Adam.

Adriana and Unitus went home and climbed into bed and held each other. The kids were asleep.

They got the call from Madeline that Janice had the little boy, and his name was Andy. They are doing well. Adam and she are sleeping now. Eunice will not rest, but I would be the same. Trevor is sleeping in a recliner and I am going to join him until you two get here," Madeline said.

Marcus was holding his own.

Tate and Debbie were helping with the babies. As were Beatrice and Kyleigh. Roscoe and Guy had the older kids occupied. Cowboys and Indians was a fun "new" game for them.

Bruce and Jana went to the hospital to relieve Madeline and Trevor. Bruce went to see Adam, and Jana went to be with Eunice. Adriana and Unitus had not awakened yet, because they had been up all night.

The ones to worry about was Jason and Cheri, Corey and Ellen were left out of the loop. So they were going today to the hospital to help do something.

Ellen and Cheri were so excited to see the baby and Janice.

Adam was so excited to see Corey and Jason to show them ... his boy. They finally got the story from Adam about what had happened. "So many unanswered questions."

"Marcus is a good man," Jason said. "This has about killed him." He wish he hadn't said it, but it was the truth.

"Unitus said he was going to be his lawyer and clear his name for us not to worry," Adam said.

"Finally Marcus knew we cared!" Jason was sharing.

"He told me we were his family," Jason continued. "MY Mom loves Marcus ... so much! My dad died so Marcus can't die, too. It would kill her."

Now he had said it, better out than inside eating away at him.

His new bride Cheri hugged him. She knew Jason had not slept a wink.

While the people were at the hospital, the three new men at Marcus's were not guards at all. Lonestar saw them taking things from the house. He called the FBI quickly because Trevor was at the hospital. He had to do it himself.

They moved in on them, and shut them down. They were actually JEWEL thieves sent to wipe Marcus out, and use the money for drug trafficking. Lonestar recognized Jung's MO.

"Lonestar you are on the ball, man! Why don't you come work for us! Sterling said. "The FBI needs good men!"

"I did my time. I am just here to help a friend out. NO one had better LIE on him like they did on Mr. Buchanan, or they will have to deal with me. You can put that in your report! You people got your facts mixed up by the wrong people. Jung had that man say that and you know it! Why don't you do something that makes sense and CLEAR the man's name while he is fighting for his life and the life of his family!" He walked off, leaving Sterling and his agents standing with their mouths open. They had NEVER heard Lonestar say a word. It was always to Trevor that he talked.

"This is a good thing. He made sense." They put their heads together to see what they could do. "To err is human!"

CHAPTER THREE

Nothing had changed with Marcus. He was still in ICU. Eunice was there every hour to visit ten minutes, talk to him and rub his hand. Adriana would sit with her or Madeline.

There was a celebration of life a couple of floors down. The new father was beaming and the new mother was holding her own. They had to do a C-section because of her prior pelvic injuries. They were told it would be safer for the mother and the baby.

Adam stated at the nursery glass, "I am going to need everyone of you to help me through this. I know nothing about babies."

The older nurse walked by and Roscoe winked at her, and she said, "I will teach you EVERYTHING that you want to know about babies!"

She stopped and winked at Roscoe, "And he will teach you everything else, but you may end up with triplets! So be careful who you talk to, Sonny!" she hurried back to work.

"She is right! She is the pro. Help deliver all seven of mine! She took good care of me when I hit the floor," Roscoe had to pat Adam on the back to get him to breath because he was laughing so hard.

Corey, Tate, and Jason were taking it all in. Corey said, "Guess we three musketeers will be next!" Jason said, "No way!" Corey said, "We can't afford any!" Tate said, "We don't WANT any!" because Debbie was sterile.

The family was gathered at the hospital and Beatrice, Kyleigh, and Debbie were caring for the children. Guy hung back and pretended to be working, but mainly wanted to be around to show Kyleigh she was going to have his protection.

Lonestar had stopped to speak to him about what had happened. "Tell Trevor before Miss Eunice goes home. That's a tough little woman with her brother about blowing her up at the restaurant and now this. Losing her first husband like I lost my wife, I hope ... Marcus makes it. I got to be going. If you' all need me, Trevor knows how to get me."

He was gone before Guy could turn back around.

Trevor wished he had not missed his friend's leaving, but that was like Lonestar. "Guy I am sorry. We have left you to the women, but you are the man for the job."

"Madeline needs a rest, but she won't leave Eunice. She said if it was me, she'd be there for her. I need to sleep a couple of hours. Will you wake me?" Trevor asked and Guy nodded.

Guy asked, "Anything else I can do for you?"

Trevor said, "Feed the horses and the dogs!"

"No problem. Get some rest," Guy said and gave him a hug. Trevor went into his bedroom and laid down.

A tired soul was he. If anything happened to Marcus, he would have to officiate. "That is weighing heavy on my heart, O 'Lord!" he said to himself. "Give me strength!" and he fell asleep.

Guy let him sleep three hours, and said he got busy and apologized for not calling him in the two hours.

Madeline came home next and slept three hours. They had alternated for days, and Marcus was finally off the ventilator.

He still was not able to talk. The doctor did not want him out of ICU yet, and wanted him to have only a few visitors. "I don't want him getting upset that will put a strain on his heart. Just the wife and daughter for right now only ten minutes at a time." They all agreed.

Adriana was being held by Unitus whom had to tell her about the three thieves. "I don't think Eunice would even know if anything is missing. The kids have been here at the hospital with Adam and Janice, and visiting Eunice. They may not have even realize it," he said. She nodded.

"Let's walk a little there is something else I think that may pan out." Unitus didn't want to get her hopes up, but felt this may boost her spirits. They sat in the atrium on a bench and he held her.

"Lonestar left today. He is who tracked the thieves down. He is a wonderful man. HE told a few people off on his way out of town," Unitus was grinning at her.

She was coming to life, "You're kidding? And ?" she punched him asking. "Come on and tell me?"

"He told Sterling and the FBI agents that they had accused the wrong man. Jung put that in that man's mouth. Mr Marcus is a fine man. They had better fess up to their mistake and make it right! He said it better than I!" Unitus stated. She was smiling, kissed him in front of everyone and sat in his lap.

"Oh no! You cannot do that! Oh no no!" he got up and walked fast to the men's bathroom, throwing water in his face.

Looking in the mirror he said, "Women got it made. They can cover everything up!" and he looked down.

The man beside him said, "You are so right!" he looked down. "Geez!" and he ran out without zipping up.

Adriana had gone back to get Eunice to come and eat in the cafeteria with her, and Madeline who had just got back.

Unitus went to check on Adam and Janice. They were to take the baby home today. Trevor was there, and he told them to bring the baby on over to their house, if they had any problems.

"There's plenty of baby sitters there. The K & B experienced team of Know- It- All s!" he laughed.

"They know it ALL about babies!" Janice said, "Thank you so much. We may come over soon," and she looked at Adam.

Adam said, "When I get back to work I'd feel so much better, if someone was with them. I appreciate it. Aunt Eunice is going to have her hands full with Mr. Marcus."

Trevor hugged them all. Ellen and Debbie rode with Janice, Adam and "Little Andy" in the white limo which Mr. Trevor insisted on them taking.

Tate, Corey, and Jason followed them in Jason's jeep.

The security guards of Marcus's original crew were in place and welcomed them. They had been briefed not to upset the family with details of the happenings while they had been at the hospital.

Janice had had to stay a couple extra days because of the C-section and her recovery time was longer due to her pain. She had to take medication to go to sleep at night. She was sleeping without those now, and happy to go home.

Unitus was walking the halls when Trevor met him, "Come let's eat with the women in the cafeteria. You have got to be starving. I know I am!"

They sat around the large round table and were chatting when "Code Blue Cardiac Floor Room 431! Code Blue Cardiac Floor Room 431!" They all froze. Eunice was pale and said, "That is not his room number!"

Everyone breathed a sigh of relief. "Madeline if you don't care, I would like to stay with you and get a good night's sleep. The boys and girls can stay at my house."

"Sounds like a good idea, honey. You are always welcome!"

Adriana said, "Daddy would want you there with us," and hugged Eunice.

Unitus and Trevor waited for James, escorted the women into the limo, and they went home. The last visiting hour was eight PM. Marcus was stable, so Eunice needed to take care of herself. Finally, she'd get some much needed rest.

All the kids were in bed. Tate and Debbie stayed at Corey and Ellen's insistence after learning Eunice would not be there. They could have a fun young couples' night.

Until the baby cried, and Adam handed Andy to Janice to breastfeed. She sat facing away from the others, and Adam sat in front of her watching his son latch on to his wife's breast.

He had the warmest feeling in his heart. He did not have to wash bottles or sterilize them, and all that junk.

Thank God Janice had ample milk, and the nurses had taught her everything to care for the baby and her nipples. Those gorgeous nipples. "That is one lucky little boy. I would love to be in his place right now. He should sleep good tonight. That was a good meal, Andy."

He held him saying, "I sure did love watching you eat, boy! One day I am going to feast on them maybe in," he growled. "About six weeks! I am going to say move over son!" He was staring at Janice who was holding a pillow to her abdomen and laughing painfully.

"Anyone wants to hold the baby. Wash your hands!" and he laughed. "That is what my teacher nurse said to say. I got to tote my beautiful wife to bed." He scooped her up and carried her to their bedroom. He came back to get the baby and put him in the bassinet beside her.

He said, "Been fun... but this poppa is going to bed. Behave yourselves!" and he showered and slide into bed beside Janice who was now sleeping snuggled in his arms. He said a prayer for Marcus. It was good to be home, and in his own bed with his family in this room. He drifted off to sleep.

In four hours he hear a baby crying, and Janice could not get up without the side rails on the bed. He got up and handed him to her and got a diaper. He was going to change his first diaper.

The little fellow peed all over him.

Janice said, "You know you are going to have to clean that up partner."

Adam said, "I know but I finally got one on him. Ain't it cute?" She grabbed the pillow and was laughing so hard.

"Honey, you only have one leg taped. If he pooped it would be EVERYWHERE. Let's try it again and cover him while you are changing him."

He said, "That's what I did and that's how only one leg got taped. The other one was under the cover!"

Janice could not stop laughing. "Now I got to have a pain pill. I have missed you making me laugh!"

He held up his right hand and said, "I swear, I am not. I'm just new at this. Give me a few days and see who's laughing."

Adam gave her her medicine and slipped under the covers, and drew her carefully into his arms, and kissed her neck.

"Stop before I have to hurt you," Janice said.

"OK but there is a revolt a brewing!" Adam said.

"I know it. I feel it on the back of my leg," and grabbed the pillow to laugh again.

"If you don't let me sleep some ... you will have to nurse the baby next go round."

He got up and walked around the bed so he could see her eyes. "They didn't teach me that one. What do I do?"

"Go to sleep. I was only kidding," she said. "I have two babies now! Go to sleep little baby."

"I want to be rocked. Please rock me, baby," he said.

"I will rock you tomorrow!" she said.

"You will! WOW!" he said.

"In that chair over there. It's called a rocker-glider," she told him. He said, "Sounds like what I want to do to you."

"I will get my pumps out tomorrow, and you will have milk for the baby bottles."

She added, "MEN!" She was tired.

Unitus went by the courthouse and got some papers about Marcus's case and everything he could get while he was there.

He grabbed his spare briefcase and jacket. He saw Sterling, and he closed the door behind them.

"Seems I have uncovered so much dirt on this fellow Tito that he is spilling his guts. Amazing what a few thumbscrews will do! Just kidding!" He winked at the overhead camera.

"I've got enough and will present it to the judge. The case will definitely be dismissed. We have all Marcus's business records, and throughout the years everything has been above board. I hope he knows I had to follow procedure," Sterling said.

Unitus asked if he could have a copy of everything about Marcus and about Tito. "Bring it to Trevor's and I will get it!"

Unitus wanted this information before he lambasted him.

Marcus may want to sue them for causing his heart attack. Definitely he could prove Marcus would not have had one, if it were not for his arrest. It definitely caused bodily harm.

Unitus's mind was working overtime to prove this could and this would have been avoided, if the FBI had done their homework prior to the arrest. Marcus would have been at home sipping on a martini.

Hindsight was a bitch. It would be Marcus's decision after the charges are dismissed, not his.

He had everything he had came for. He locked their office back. Adriana and his office, both were the town DAs.

They had many valuable books in there and no one had permission to enter.

If the assistant DA Brandon Trueheart needed anything about any case, all he had to do was email him. He had everything in folders on his laptop, and could send them with one click. He also could pull up from his phone and send.

Therefore no need for Brandon to be nosing around in their stuff. She had the office for six months, and he had the office the other six months … each spending time with the kids. Their partnership was well received by the court, and the people of this district were supportive of their hard work.

He took the briefcase home with him that night. He and Adriana discussed the case. Which made her horny, "I just love it when you talk dirty." Any legal jargon was a turn on.

She was feeding Vanderbilt saying things like that. He put the briefcase down.

"So that is why I haven't been getting any? You wanted me to woo you from the prosecutor's aspect that this body has been harmed intentionally by said plaintiff such as yourself, and I have been duly denied compensation for my injuries!"

"Stop counselor, I concur. I have been negligent and must compensate you. I will throw myself at the mercy of the court if you put our son to bed while I shower. Angel is sleeping and the tension is building as the two opposing parties are settling out of court. This has been mutually agreed upon, and you have signed on the dotted line, Mister!" Adriana smiled.

Their night was exactly what both had been needing, and the next morning the others were commenting on how rested they looked.

Only they knew that they had barely slept a wink!

CHAPTER FOUR

Beatrice and Kyleigh were finally able to go back home and spread their wings. It was a joyous time to finally get the kids settled back into their own rooms.

Madison said he was going to miss his cousins.

She told him, "Honey they are just next door. You see them every day at school."

"I know Mommy, but we can't play at school, and they have all those after school activities," she hugged him.

Kyleigh pouted her lips, "I guess you think I'm no fun any more?"

Guy grabbed her around the waist, "You are always fun Mommy."

"I was talking to Madison," and Madison hugged her, too.

"You are fun Mommy and I love you!" Madison went to his room and started getting his homework done.

Guy was working on his homework as best he could.

Kyleigh was fighting him playfully, and declaring her intention to pay him back for his display in front of Madison.

"I have to go by the office for a little while and pick up a few things. I won't be long!" He left in the Land Rover and returned with his briefcase, and a dozen red roses.

"That is so sweet and I will reward you tonight. I have something to show you after I put these in water."

She had a package that she had ordered. She unwrapped a red teddy lingerie and held it up, "I thought you might like!"

"Uncle Tate and Aunt Debbie are going to stay with us while Eunice is at the hospital, honey! I have got to get back to work or we will have no customers," Adam kissed Janice and Andy, and ran out the door. He had stayed home for a week and his two repairmen Bernard and Lopez, had kept the business going.

Adam hated to leave this morning, but he would leave work at five and have the evening to fuss over them. He called her twice and she was feeling better.

Debbie had been cooking nutritious meals, and Janice was getting stronger. Tate had anchored a side-rail to her bed, and she could get up by herself and get little Andy out of the bassinet. She just couldn't get out of that glider chair yet.

Cheri helped as did Ellen, while Corey and Jason were at work. Jason had found a job at a computer shop, and he was enjoying making some money, and going to school twice weekly at night. He sure did miss his mom.

Marcus was getting better. He was up walking the hall twice a day. Madeline and Trevor were still helping to get Eunice back and forth. She was still staying with them, and she confided to Madeline.

"I just can't go in that big house without Marcus. I would never sleep a wink in that big bed without him."

She called Jason and Corey everyday. They said they understood, and they went by the hospital to see Marcus most every day.

He really enjoyed their visits. He called them HIS boys. As he did Adam, who took him pictures of the baby and Janice.

Jasmine called Madeline and she told her about the happenings. Trevor spoke to her and told her to come on home, if she wanted. "The coast is clear."

"We have enough security and the raid took most of the Jung's clan out. It is for you and John to decide, but we sure do miss you," Trevor told her.

"I want to come home. John wants to build there near you guys. What do you think of that?" Jasmine asked.

"That would be wonderful. I have a piece of property for you to see. It can be your wedding present. If you and John like it, we will get started on it when you come home!"

"My phone is about to die. Tell everyone hello and we send our love. Bye for now!" and the phone went dead.

She looked at John and he wrapped his arms around her and said, "Let's go home."

They got in the truck and Clancy was howling. He loved to ride. They were going to miss the farm. The spring was almost here and every room in the farmhouse had a painting that she had painted.

She signed them all J & J … for Jasmine and John. They would leave them for others to enjoy.

They decided to take the truck so Clancy could go with them. It would take at least three or four days. They could not abandon him. He had been abandoned when they found him in that shelter. They couldn't do that to him again. He was a part of their family now. John loved him as much as she did.

It was going to be a long journey, but knowing that family was waiting with open arms made it worth it!

The private school did not have a principal. Jackson Private Academy nestled in the Blue Ridge Mountains was the school that Bruce had interviewed for the math position. He had been turned down by the drug selling Glen Robertson due to being overqualified. Glen knew Bruce would get him.

Now that he was behind bars, the school needed a principal. The faulty had reviewed his application and felt he WAS qualified for THIS job position, principal.

He had done excellent in English in high school and college. Planning & Management in the military was a given. Teamwork and Execution of strategies for projects were commendable. His legal status was in limbo but it was not a blemish because people in these parts of the country understood about the school bus explosion and all the problems his family had gone through with Jared Banks. His CIA report was confidential, but carried more weight than anything else. His record was honorable discharge.

His being even considered, spoke volumes.

He was asked in this letter, if he would be interested. If so, please contact the school and ask for Dennis Newton.

He would talk to Jana tonight. She may go for it or she may not. It was something they together would talk about. Being a teacher, he could go home and have regular hours. A principal's obligations may take a lot of time away from her. Would it be worth the commitment, that was the question?

"Jana would you like to be wined and dined tonight?" Bruce was baiting the hook.

"Of course, what woman wouldn't?" she smiled slightly.

She put her white kimono on with the cherry blossoms that Bruce loved so much. It always reminded them of their honeymoon. She smiled more as he helped her into the limo.

He had spoken with Trevor, and he had suggested it. They would be at the hospital later on, and did not need it till eight.

Since this was an early supper at THE INN, he had wore his casual khakis and blue shirt. Spring had sprung, and the weather was delightful... not too hot... and not too cold.

Jana said, "I know you are after something and I don't care! I love it when you surprise me," she patted the side of his face before they walked in.

She did that to let him know she could slap that face just as easily.

She was already turning him on with her charm. Her subtle enticements. Her porcelain white legs were being displayed as she slid into a cozy secluded corner booth.

They always sat close when dining. She asked, "Does this have anything to do with that letter you received from that school? I did notice it on the dresser when we left."

"You are so observant. I can't get a thing pass you nor do I want to. Yes, but let's eat first and then we can talk later."

"You know I can't wait until later," she rubbed her stocking toe up and down his shin adding, "We will have other things to do later."

Staring into her eyes, "You are so right! They want me to apply for the principal's position that just came open. Do you have any objections?"

"None at all," she said and he sealed it with a kiss.

Jana said, "There is one thing!"

"What my dear?" he stop eating looking at her puzzled.

"We won't be able to stop by the road and have a quickie because all the kids will recognize you. Nor can we go into that service station bathroom together, and do important things," she grinned.

"Are you saying, we will be boring after all these years together?" he could not wait to hear her answer to that.

"My dear Bruce have you ever know US to be boring?" she stated as fact.

"We will have to plan well, and not be as spontaneous in public as we usually are. That is a respectable position that carries a lot of restriction to protect the minds of children," and she put her toes in her shoes.

"You are right. We do get x-rated occasionally darling, and I think we need to get home fast. My mind is loving you already. Waiter! Waiter! Check please!"

Bruce was really having a moment and Jana was giggling and covering her face.

"You are not helping," he said with a grin.

"Oh, I will be helping myself pretty soon," she said.

"Of course James may not be surprised, but I'm locking the doors, pulling the privacy screen down and having those gorgeous legs around me now!"

Jana had no undies on, "When you said dine, I knew it was me … you would dine on. I came prepared."

CHAPTER FIVE

Eunice was all smiles as Marcus was asking her for a kiss.

"You still love me and believe in me?" he asked.

"I will always believe in you. I knew they had done a terrible thing when they accuse you of all people. You are the nicest, kindest person, I have ever met!" and she kiss him.

The three musketeers Corey, Jason and Tate came in now that he had a private room.

Jason relayed, "Adam said he wanted to come, but he had to babysit." He laughed and showed Marcus the pictures of Adam putting on a diaper, feeding the baby, and rocking him in the rocker-glider chair. He was making comedic faces in all of the pictures. It made Marcus laugh.

It had been six weeks since Marcus had had the heart attack. Six weeks five hours thirty minutes since the birth!

But who's counting. Adam was!

He was doing everything today to keep his mind off Janice.

She was looking so good and those breasts were huge. He had to stop before he left his work unfinished. He finally told Bernard, "I got to go. You close up. I'm feeling sick!"

He sped home and surprised Janice.

"Is something wrong?" she had a frightened look on her face.

"No honey," and kissed her and bent her over the sofa and was taking his clothes off.

"Hey you two must want to be alone," Ellen came out of the kitchen covering her eyes and grabbing her purse.

"Smart girl!" Adam had Janice in his arms.

"How long has Andy been a sleep?" as he took the remaining clothes off her and himself.

"Two minutes. Are you in a hurry or something?" she asked.

"No, I'd say I have been patient and you did say six weeks. Well today is six weeks! OH my, you are as ready as me!" Adam felt her moisture and eased in, and pulled out.

"What are you doing? Bring it back. I have wanted it for the last two weeks bad and you know it." She was pulling on his shoulders and he came back.

"I am not going to be easy because I am almost over the edge right now."

"It is what I want and need. You will not hurt me. I might get pregnant, but that is the chance we take when you breastfeed. No birth control pills because it may harm the baby. We gotta take that chance! Don't think just HURRY!" she was just about there herself.

He was two strokes and she was done. He was four and holding. She moved and he took them both to the apex and they came down at the same time.

"That was so special darling! You know we made a girl," Adam said as he lay sweating and in a happy place at four in the afternoon.

"Andy needs a sister. Do you feel like it again? I am exploding with warmth just for you," Adam moaned.

"Thirty minutes, Andy awakens!" she said licking his lips.

Roscoe was dealing with two thirteen year old boys, his first born wanted to play some pool with two girls in their class.

"We won't be long. Haley's dad will be there. It's his pool table. Is it okay?" Cain asked.

Caleb swatted his brother on the shoulder, "We got to go Dad! Will you take us?"

"Sure. I want to meet Haley's dad. I think I have his number in my phone," He was flipping through his contacts. "Bingo there it is!"

"You 'all go get in the truck. I'll be there in just a minute," Roscoe said and they ran outside.

"Now what are we going to do?" Cain asked.

"I don't know. If Dad calls him, he is going to be mad. Whoa! Haley is going to rip my head off!"

"Why?" Caleb asked innocently. Candy was his girlfriend and she was not involved with Cain's lie.

"You shouldn't have told him that her dad would be there."

"Do you really think he would let us go, if her dad was NOT there?"

"He would say now boys you could get you into a lot of trouble. Girls at your age are trouble," Cain acted out the mannerisms of his father.

"Girls at any age are trouble," Beatrice said.

"Ain't that the truth," Roscoe was looking at his pale green eyed wife. Just wondering what she had them planned for the night. Since that famous vasectomy, she was an animal.

"Now boys, you could get into a lot!" Roscoe did his speech.

"That was a good try fellas," Roscoe walked around looking each one in the eyes.

"I give you credit. It almost worked. Now go to your rooms and call the girls. Tell them Haley's father knows. She is going to be grounded as you two are for a week," he said.

Roscoe was looking at Beatrice, and smiling because he was going to take her on their ride over the hill tonight. It was their date night.

She was grinning because she knew what he was thinking.

"These boys and their hormones!" Roscoe said.

"Oh man of mine, is your testosterone getting high?" she asked so meekly.

He said, "Have you seen your husband when it was not?" he asked grimacing as if his load was heavy.

"You are such a hypocrite. Those boys are just like their father," Beatrice walked toward him.

Waving his hands, "Stay away for God's sake. Don't come near me!"

"That is no way to talk to the woman of your dreams," and she blew him an air kiss that hit him below the belt and she walked off.

"She is right again! They are just like me and that worries me. So I have to give them ... the dreaded TALK," he said to himself and it was going to be painful.

"The teacher told us that in third grade, Dad," Cain said.

"And fifth grade and seventh grade! Unless something has changed? We're knowledgeable in that area!" Caleb added.

"Nope, nothing has changed anatomically," Roscoe admitted.

Roscoe asked Beatrice if she had given their twelve year old twin girls, the TALK. She said, "Why yes years ago."

He sat in a daze, "Am I the only one that didn't get the TALK till I was sixteen and it was from grandma?"

"Woe is me!" Roscoe was getting a pat on the back from Beatrice.

She said, "It is a different era now! They no everything!"

Roscoe said, "Well it sure DOESN'T look like it when they bring home their report cards."

"Honey, they remember what they want to remember," she puckered up for a kiss. "I talked to the triplets, too!"

He started waving his hands again.

"You are driving me crazy, woman!" Roscoe repeated.

"I know it's my job! It came with the title!" she said.

"What title?" he asked.

"Wife," and she smiled at him and blew him another kiss.

He could hardly wait for their date. She was dressed in the cutest mint green jumpsuit with white flats. Her hair, she had pulled the red curls up with a white clasp. Peach lip gloss completed her sexy look.

Roscoe said, "You look good enough to eat!"

Beatrice said, "That is one of my wishes."

"Your wish is my command. I must fulfill all your wishes before the night is through," he declared.

They drove to their hideaway and he took her jumpsuit off. He knew there would be nothing underneath. She took his jeans and shirt off for him and folded them, and then her wish came true. After she hollered, mission accomplished.

Jasmine and John were in route with Clancy their hound dog. It was their third day. They had slept in the truck bed since it was summer, and tied Clancy to the bumper.

All their belongings were in a small U-haul behind them, and they had their hibachi grill handy for cooking breakfast and dinner. They did not want to stop at any major city for fear someone would spot them.

Even though their close up appearance had changed at a distance, their profiles were the same.

"I can hardly wait to take a shower instead of washing in a service station bathroom," she laughed out loud.

"We could go skinny dipping in the middle of the day in the stream. I saw one back up the road, Love?" John asked with his dreamy eyes begging.

"Do you think it safe? I hate snakes," she cringed and visibly shivered.

"I guess that is a NO!" and he rubbed Clancy's head.

"When we build and have a swimming pool, I promise we can go skinny dipping any day and every day you want my darling. I have to see my toes!" smiling but she COULDN'T swim and she'd tell him later.

He jumped out of the truck and pulled her off the tailgate and into his arms. "That sounds like a wonderful idea and I can hardly wait until then! We need to figure out how I can keep from ravishing you on the side of this highway."

Cars were passing by honking their horns. "Oh get a life!" John shouted at one screwball and continued to seduce her.

It was working until Clancy started barking which brought them back to reality. He never barked when they were kissing or ... He only barked when someone was near.

The Tennessee highway patrol officer said, "Good day, folks. Hate to interrupt, but you two need to be moseying on along down the road. Got a few complaints from parents with small children that said it was inappropriate activity going on, on the side of this road," he furrowed his brow.

"I understand officer. We were just fixing to leave. We're NEWLYWEDS!" and John flashed him his left ring finger.

"Oh Okay, that explains the behavior. You 'all have a good day! Congratulations! Me and the missus were the same way hmm ... fifteen years ago." He walked back to his patrol car and drove off.

"We will continue this tonight in our old bed. It will be six hours, but I can't hardly wait. You hold that thought just don't reach for anything while I am driving or we may get arrested," he grinned at her.

"Can't promise a thing," Jasmine grabbed her sketch pad.

She was as horny as he. They had never been this long without making mad passionate love.

Clancy was laying upside down in the back cab stretched out with his jowls flapping in the wind, and looking at them as if to say you are not going to use my bed for such as that.

He was real territorial about the backseat.

John said, "If something happens and we shouldn't get home tonight," he laughed.

"I may have dog bites on my arse because I am going in that backseat with you, Lady!" swerving to miss a car.

"Mark my words!" he was talking while no cars were in front of him.

"I'll be looking forward to the brawl between you and Clancy. I'll just get me a bag of popcorn at the next pit stop. A good fight always makes me hungry!" Jasmine laughed.

John's eyes were twinkling with excitement. It was strange how she affected him with just a few words after all this time. She could arouse him so quickly. She would not. No she would not… he told himself as they sat at the rest stop.

She did it. She reached for him, and he lost it.

He grabbed her, "You just had to push it!" He cranked up the truck, and pulled as far away from the other cars as he could.

Pulling sideways up against the curb instead of pulling straight in because he wanted no one behind them.

He got out and open her door. She turned and asked, "What are you doing?" as if she didn't know and her breathing was increasing.

"You had better scoot over here. If you want this?" and he showed her what she had been asking for. She took her jeans off quickly and lay down and scooted to the edge of the seat and he filled her. He was forcing her to moan so loudly that Clancy was looking out the back window as if he were their guard dog.

John brought her on to him fully and they meshed, and they stared into each others' eyes as the cadence started. Nothing mattered, but their need. He was waiting as long as he could and he felt it happen for her, and he sped up until his head went back. All was sate, and he was coming to his senses.

He said, "You are the best thing that has ever happened to me. Just don't move, please! Because these people are going to get a better show. Next time, I will be. I am going to be on the top of this truck!"

"We will be home soon. I will behave, but don't expect me to be so submissive when I get there," she smiled as she squeezed, and turned away from him.

"We could have not made it home without this," she was washing and he was watching. He toweled off and looked at Clancy who was chewing on his large bone. The one they had bought him at the last stop.

"We gotta go and I'm hungry!" he said.

"You got to be kidding?" she looked at him sideways. "Hungry for food my dear wife. Hungry for FOOD!" he said.

"I'm not cooking tonight. I am cooked out," she sighed.

"Good! I did my job right, and that should hold us till we get home," he was stretching to emphasis his chest size.

"Proud as a peacock. Aren't you?" and she reached for him.

"Clancy help! Protect me, she has gone crazy!" John grinned and Jasmine got in the truck.

She was sitting in the back with Clancy, "Happy now?"

"No Ma'am, but I have my eye on you," he was adjusting his rear-view mirror.

The dog was howling as they traveled down the road to North Carolina.

PART TWENTY TWO

CHAPTER ONE

The three jewel thieves were still in the county jail. One was a Mexican named Hernandez. He had been an undercover cop for a year. He was deep into Jung 's gang of trusted employees because he had proven himself. He had convinced them that he was worthy of this job assignment.

Eunice did not realize that the necklace Marcus had given her for Christmas was made of rubies and diamonds worth a half million dollars.

He had kept it in his wall safe along with several other pieces of jewelry, he had given her. Some were worth more.

This is why the thieves were at his house at Jung's request. As he sat in his cell Jung dictated everything his men did on the outside. He laughed to himself, "I chose wisely the right men." He tested and retested all his men for loyalty. "The Mexican has not failed me yet."

Since the incarceration, Hernandez had given all the details of months of investigation into Jung's organization in his in- depth report. He told his superiors that they needed to seize and attack. "Before Jung gets wind of this failed caper."

Hernandez would have to stay in jail with the others or the main sting would falter. He laid his life on the line to catch Jung, and KEEP him behind bars. Why? because Jung had beheaded his cousin. He promised his family. He will pay.

He wanted his vengeance against Jung. He could not go to any prison though. He would not go there, but he would stay at this jail because he was covered by his team.

The other two had been interrogated as they thought he had.

They were talking and he hoped they were speaking the truth for his report's validation.

The two others were Vinny, an Italian brass knuckle idiot that beat people up that could not pay Jung drug monies. The other was Swinn, a Scandinavian immigrant who loved to mutilate people who could not pay for drug monies.

They both had done jewel heist for Jung. Hernandez was the new kid on the block and they were afraid of him because he did an execution style murder for Jung. One of the murderers of Jung had to be wasted.

Because he was a man identified as one of the men that had killed his cousin, Hernandez had no problem pulling the trigger and he laughed afterward in Swinn and Vinny's faces.

That was the main reason Jung chose Hernandez because he was deadly.

Jung said, "Get the jewels and if you have to waste Swinn and Vinny do it." They had no idea what Jung was asking.

His response, "No problem Master Jung!"

As he sat in the cell with them, he was eyeing them, and they him. Each of them did not trust the other, and Hernandez definitely didn't trust either of them.

"What's the next move? Will Jung send a lawyer or are we on our own," Hernandez asked.

"Never! He wants us to kill each other!" Swinn said. "If we don't, he will have us killed. Who wants to go first?"

Vinny said, "I think you should be first Swinn!" and he stabbed him with a shank.

Hernandez said, "Don't try it asshole!"

"Wasn't going to! The guards will be here in a minute, so take the shank!" and he did. It would get him into solitary where he needed to be. His team would get him out.

When out into the interrogation room, he told them what happened. He said, "I am done. I have done my duty. This man killed Swinn and he will try me, and I don't want to kill him. I want his information and you want his information. So do your job!"

"Hi aye Captain," and they gave him a disguise and he had gone back to his family. His wife Margarita was so relieved to see her husband. It had been a year since she had seen him and she had not known whether he was dead or alive.

"Le amo," "I love you," his wife said. In came his children Veronica, Juana, Miguel and Jose. "Me encanta padre!" "I love you father!"

All hugs and kisses. Much love was expressed and the children were ushered out. There would be time for family later, and the older ones kept the little ones busy as madre had requested.

Hernandez had eyes for only Margarita. He was dirty and unshaven, and his hair was long. She bathe him and shaved him, and tied his hair back. She said nothing, just disrobed.

There was nothing to say except "te quiero" "I love you no matter what!" Margarita said.

He puts his arms around her and said, "Necesito que!" "I need that!" and pressed her to his manhood. They disappeared for four hours and came to eat. They went back into their room. Not to come out until the next morning.

He could not tell her what he had done, but that it was for his work as an undercover policeman. She was so proud of him. He could say, "Juan will rest in peace." Juan was his cousin that had died at Jung's hands.

He had no regrets other than his life was to be in disguise at all times. No one at his job knew he was married. They lived in Mexico, and he traveled back and forth to see them.

He had to be careful so no one could find out. It was for his family's safety. He would stay home for almost a year and then return to his job in America. He could not stay away an entire year so these ten months were going to be packed with much love and devotion. Probably a new child which Margarita had wanted another. "Then no more," she said laughing.

She was roasting a pig in the ground, potatoes, corn on the cob were also cooked in this fashion. The large olla of beans was on the stove. The family would feast and celebrate with their extended families.

All that knew Hernandez would come and bring food with them, and join in the homecoming.

The kids would burst the pinata, and gather the candy and toys that spilled to the ground.

Margarita's joy was bright.

It was a happy time for Hernandez and his family.

Eunice said, "I cannot believe I will finally be able to sleep in my own bed."

Marcus said, "I cannot believe I will finally be able to put you to bed," and he laughed.

He was leaving the hospital today. His limo had come to pick them up with body guards in place.

The family was anxious for him to be home and they had planned a nice dinner with Debbie and Tate 's help.

Madeline and Trevor were going to give them time to adjust before they went over. They were actually going to spend time with their own family, and prepare for Michelle and Robert … aka… Jasmine and John's return.

She told Trevor that they maybe late getting in, but they would all be here to welcome them home tonight whatever time.

The kids were so use to going back and forth. They had all the clothes they would need at either home, and knew where their rooms were.

Madeline said they are getting so big, "Who has been feeding these kids The Jolly Green Giant?"

Roscoe said, "'Twas you GM !" and he smiled. "Best food in town! Where is that Debbie?"

"She is cooking for her second family. Marcus came home today! Thank goodness with our Jasmine coming home. I wanted to prepare a meal and be at home myself," she smiled at Trevor.

"And be with the ones I love the most!" Madeline said.

They all said, "Here! Here!"

In walks Jasmine and John and Clancy which had the Black Russian terriers on a barking rampage.

Jasmine was hugging everyone and John was hugging, and holding Clancy's leash tightly. He was getting all the rubbing and petting a dog should have for a lifetime.

"Sorry! He is like an old shoe you park by the fireplace, and he stays there. Hope the Black Russians like him. We found him at a shelter and Jasmine fell in love with him as she did me," John smiled widely at her.

Jasmine said, "Would it be possible, if we go and shower?Been four days and I know we reek!"

"Of course, you 'all go to YOUR room and we will set the table," Madeline said smiling and laughing like she had not done in a long while.

Trevor was sitting with Clancy firmly attached to him by the fire. With John's quick return, he could not stay in that room with his wife naked … showering.

When she finished, he would go back.

John found Clancy, "I see, I have competition."

"He seems to like the family and kids that is hard to find," Trevor said.

"Jasmine has tamed the creature. Just like she did me," and he grinned.

"Madeline and I are so glad you two are home and while I have you a few moments alone. I want us to go look at a piece of land next door tomorrow, and get this show on the road!" Trevor said.

"Sounds like music to my ears, sir!" John said as Jasmine came around the corner and took his breath away.

He had forgotten how gorgeous she was when she dressed up. In that beautiful cashmere camel sweater with no bra and plaid slacks that fit her every curve to perfection. Her own hair color a dark brown with red natural highlights tied in a caramel colored ribbon in the back that was so chic. He gulped.

Those violet eyes with black mascara and peach lip gloss unnerved him. She was standing so tall in those three inch heels next to him, and smelled of CIARA. His mouth was wide open.

She said, "Close your mouth honey and go get a shower. I'm hungry!" not turning to look him in the eyes.

He went flying down the hall. She had said in just those two words "I'm hungry" that she was lusting after him. No one knew it, but him. Their definition of hunger was different than most people. Most people thought of food, but not them.

He showered and shaved except for a tiny mustache like he had when they first met. He put on the English Leather cologne that she loved.

He had use it last time he was here, and it had turned her on something fierce. He had to make a statement, too. So he got his black suit pants and black dress boots of soft leather that she loved to rub. Pulled on a gray cashmere turtleneck that showed his massive chest and abs indentures.

He had blow-dried his hair in a style she that she liked. Out the door he ran, almost stumbling over Clancy. The dog was growling… he didn't recognize him.

"Jasmine honey, come get your dog!" John shouted.

"What do you mean my dog?" and she came around the corner and her eyes widened.

"Oh, I now see the problem," she said. "Come Clancy. Let's go eat. I am ravished! I am so so so hungry!" and she batted those long lashes at him.

"What problem, do you see?" John was still devouring her with his gray eyes that matched his sweater.

"Do you really want me to point out the problem in front of all these people, Honey?" she said sweetly and licked her wet lips.

She had her hand on his abs.

"Let's eat!" Jasmine whispered.

"I second the motion," and John escorted her to their room.

"You have to take me ... to the table and seat me down down and let us eat eat with ... the family!" she begged as he eased her up onto him.

"Jasmine !John! Jasmine John ! Come and eat. The foods is on the table," Madeline called.

They were inside their room and he was saying, "We have to go! You have to go. I can't!"

"Go, stay, do something!" he was begging.

"Forgive me Madeline! We are so tired from our long drive. I think we will forgo supper and get some rest, please forgive! We will make it up to you tomorrow!" Jasmine was talking through the cracked door as John was rubbing her nipples and biting the back of her neck.

"We understand dear! Just get some rest!" Madeline said.

"There is no rush now!" she said stepping out of her heels and he already had his boots off.

She said, "Feed me."

He would win every time over food. She pulled his gray sweater over his head. She felt of his abs as she unbuttoned his trousers and unzipped her present.

Meanwhile he unzipped her slacks, and they fell to the floor and he grabbed the hem of her cashmere sweater, and off it came as did her ribbon.

Her hair spilling over his chest as she kissed his nipples, and sucked in the smell of the English Leather cologne that always drove her to madness.

Her hair smelled like coconut and her skin had CIARA everywhere. He inhale her scent that drove him to madness.

Her nipples were hard and her V was wet. Then she looked into his eyes and climbed on the bed so he would kiss her navel and she could slide down him.

He waited to see how much she could take before he grabbed what she was offering.

"Oh no you don't! This is going to last a little while longer baby," he said.

"I want you to remember this night!" John stated firmly.

"But you smell so good. I am so hungry!" she grabbed him and kneaded him ever so gently, and he nibbled on her breast then suckling until she was begging.

"They are going to hear me," She moaned into his neck and he covered her mouth with his, and he was in her so fast she could hardly breathe, as the waves hit her over and over.

A never ending pleasure zone that just he knew where and how to make it last. She did know he was counting to one million and only made it ten minutes.

"Was it worth it ?" he asked.

"You looked so good I couldn't help myself," she admitted.

"I am totally weak when it comes to you," she admitted.

"Every time is simply amazing!" she sucked in air.

"I want to love you all night long!" he predicted and it was truly accurate in duration.

They consistently amaze each other.

CHAPTER TWO

Marcus was following doctor's orders and going slow. He had his team of lawyers from the business Royster, Martin, and Royster come over and review what had been happening since he had been sick.

All his affairs were in order, but his will. He wanted it drawn up that Eunice would get this house. Adriana and Unitus would get THE HOTEL and THE CASINO. All the rest of his wives would get nothing. They had not one, no not one had shown up while he was sick. Any money would be divided among Eunice, Adriana and the grandchildren of all his children. This was to be put in place this day, and he would sign it.

"Eunice I am doing this, because it never occurred to me that I would get sick. I did not have a will in place so maybe I'll live another twenty years, but then again."

He added, "Tomorrow is not promised. So I want it to be in writing, and I can sleep well at night," Marcus told her.

"If it will make you sleep better, that is the main thing," Eunice said. "I know I slept better last night."

"I am so glad," he smiled.

"Now I can tell you why I stayed at Madeline's," a tear fell down on her dress as she spoke.

"You missed me that much you couldn't sleep in our bed without me. You are the only woman that has ever said that to me," then Marcus shed a tear.

"Honey, I didn't mean to upset you," she said.

"You didn't upset me. You made me a happy man."

She kissed him, and he patted her hand that he was holding.

Bruce had called Dennis Newton and set up an appointment for an interview. Jana rode along to get out of the house. He was dressed up and looked so handsome. She dressed him to a tee. She put on one of her old business suits.

She decided to go inside and wait this time. She wanted to see what the school looked like inside, and scope out the faulty.

She wanted a school album to get a feel for the faulty. Their pictures would be in there, and so would their mission statement and goals for the school.

This would keep her reading while he was doing business.

Bruce was welcomed and Mr. Newton was friendly. The position was given to him on the spot.

He could start next week.

Jana said, "Pay the secretary or Mr. Newton for the album, Honey." Jana smiled at the new principal.

"Dennis, please call me Dennis. It's yours. No charge. Mrs Smith, ONLY the students call me Mr." and he smiled at Jana.

Bruce did a double take, "She's mine! Eyes off," and he laughed. He was going to watch this joker.

"He was just being nice Bruce. Get over it!" Jana said as they walked to the car.

"You can't start a new job with a chip on your shoulder or I won't come back here at all," she pointed out staring Bruce in his eyes.

"Good point, Jana. You are my wife, and I will let all men hit on my wife in front of me."

"That is ridiculous," she said.

"I was jealous, what can I say! I love my wife," Bruce said.

"I love my husband, and he can stay home with me!" Jana said as a matter of fact.

"You always know how to put me in my place," he said.

"I have a week to get over my jealousy and all men in that school will walk a chalk line when my wife comes to school."

"I will be studying the faculty's pictures to see ... if there are any cute little blonde women that may want to hit on my husband," and Jana winked at him.

"They don't stand a chance when I got what I want at home," Bruce grinned.

"And don't you forget that Mister Principal," and Jana laughed and snapped her fingers.

"So you are going to crack the old whip, if I am ten minutes late?" Bruce said grimacing.

"Twenty minutes I will come after you, and drag you home by the ring in your nose," she purred and he laughed.

"This is really going to spice our life up. I am getting all worked up with you talking about whips and things. Can you use handcuffs on me, too?" he fantasized.

"This is a two-way street. I want the whole nine yards when we get home," she proposed.

"We can't there is a house full," Bruce pointed out.

"It has never stopped you before?" Jana reminded him.

"But I am a principal, didn't you say yesterday that we had to set a good example for the children?"

"Jasmine and John cannot be the only two getting some. Their first night back, they couldn't even wait to eat," Bruce said.

"Are you saying you don't want supper? OK," Jana smiled.

John was looking at Jasmine and smiling.

"It is going to be hard to explain to the family that we have been alone for so long that maybe we will have to learn how to restrain our passion. That is something that I think we will not master quickly. It might take some time, what do you think?" he asked and she moved slightly.

"It will take an eternity. For my sake don't move again. For about four hours!" she requested.

They slept in the nude the whole time they were in Montana and now they were back in the mainstream. It was going to take some major adjustments.

"Dang! I forgot Trevor wants to show me some land this morning! He was so excited and after I saw my wife all dolled up, I forgot my own name again. What is it?" he asked.

"What is mine?" she had her index finger and was drawing designs on his chest and abs.

"Raven stop! Michelle Stop! Jasmine, go a little lower!"

"Robert, John Wayne go and stake a claim to that land where we can run around naked, and make our dreams come true!" pointing her finger to the door.

She laughed because she had him under her spell. He was on his back looking up at her and could not move. She had climbed on top of him to make her point.

"In a minute or two. I will do just that, but you have to stop taking advantage of my body first," he said.

She moved to get off. He stopped her midair and bench pressed her a couple of times, and settled her back where she had started a fire!

"Never leave a fire unattended. It might become a blaze and burn a house down. You got to put it out!"

Trevor and John instead of walking, saddled up the horses.

Trevor said, "I have wanted to do this for ages!"

John questioned, "Ride the horses or look at the property?"

"Both! It has been so chaotic of late, I've done neither. So glad you and Michelle, I mean Jasmine are back. Never to leave again. I have hired two bodyguards for you two. If either of you go off the property, tell them," Trevor instructed.

"They will protect you and Jasmine. While here we have all the regular security that we had before. Any questions?" Trevor had said a mouthful.

John was relieved and expressed his gratitude.

"Do you think it would be wise for me to go to my place of business yet? I have to instruct my staff on my next phase of production, and withdraw some monies for their salaries.

I had everything set up before we left, and it has worked beautifully. Now that we are back, I just don't want to delay this house that we are going to build. What do you think?"

"Hope you like it," he waved his hand as they sat on top of the hill near Unitus's and Southfork. "You can nestle in the woods or clear it all out. Whatever you decide is fine with me, but it is Michelle's and yours. Jasmine and John's, I mean. A gift from Madeline and me," Trevor looked from under his Steton that he only wore when riding his horse, Renegade.

He patted the big black stallion's neck and stared at John.

John sat and scanned the breath taking view, "It is magical. Jasmine loved the old farm house that we rented. She will be ecstatic when she sees this."

"Do you want to show her? Or me?" John asked Trevor.

"You are her husband and the love of her life. You do it!"

John got Jasmine on a horse that was a gentle pinto, and it would follow the quarter horse that John was on.

When Jasmine got on, she was timid and held onto John's hand. She loved her horse back in Montana, but she just didn't know what this one would do.

Soon she became comfortable and was laughing on the way over to the land. She had adjusted and she said, "They have got to be kidding!" Her eyes had widened in amazement at the vastness of it all. The beauty of the land above the lake.

She began crying and could not stop. He got off and tied the horses to a tree before he got her off the pinto.

"This is too much, John. My family has given too much!"

Until Madeline and Trevor the world was a cruel and unforgiving memory. Now everything they did was with loving and thoughtfulness to all their children. This solidified it, she was one of them. There was no doubt ever that they wanted her here.

"I want you to be as happy as I am. Do you want to live here with me forever?" Jasmine looked up at John and he was smiling.

"I was hoping you would say that. With those tears, you had me worried. Yes, Jazzy I want to live with you here or anywhere else in this world, but here is pure magic. The sun shining on the lake and eagles soaring onto the mountain cliff. Nowhere else would I rather be! Let's go tell Madeline and Trevor our news."

"Yes, they are waiting," and he softly kissed her.

"That's not a kiss! But you are right it. They are waiting!"

Marcus was getting exercise in the long hall every day. Janice had the baby in the stroller getting her walking exercise, also.

"Andy is a lucky fellow and so am I!" Marcus said.

Then he added whispering as if he was going to tell the baby a secret. "We don't have to go outside in the hot summer sun to walk, and we have people inside that love us."

Janice grinned and Marcus was tiring so he sat down on a bench. Janice sat down beside him.

"Can I hold the little fellow?" he asked and held him propping his arm on the armrest to steady his grip.

"This is something I missed out on with Adriana. I look back and see this is a special time. You and Adam enjoy every minute because they grow up so fast, my dear."

Marcus had done a lot of thinking while he was sick. This was one of his regrets, but Adriana still loved her father. He smiled at Janice.

"We are going to record it in pictures on a disc. So when we get older, we can look back. Would it be okay, if I take your and Andy's picture?" Janice asked.

"I'd be honored," he did not lift the baby but sat talking to him as if he understood his every word.

Andy was playing with his fingers and cooing and an occasional grin. Marcus thought it was all for him.

Janice said, "I think he likes you!" she didn't have the heart tell him the little guy was pooping in his pants.

"Janice I think he broke wind. Take him before Eunice thinks I did it!" They both laughed. "You're so funny Mr. M!"

Jason came by, "Phew something stinks!"

Marcus pointed to Andy and Janice pointed to Marcus. Both went into hysterical laughter.

Jason said, "You' all are too much for me!" and went to get Eunice because he didn't know which one was guilty.

Andy now was sounding like a motorboat Janice said, "Sorry I need to let him finish. No need to clean him up twice."

Marcus asked, "Do you mind, if I join him?"

Janice said, "Of course not!" and Marcus let a fart rip!

"Now I feel better. I was about to have another heart attack holding it!" Marcus was red faced. About that time Eunice and Adam came up, they both were in hysterical laughter. Neither could speak.

Eunice asked, "Are you two alright dear?"

Marcus said, "Never felt better!"

Adam said, "I think someone should be very proud. It's my little stinker! Yes it is!" and he picked Andy up and said he was going to go and change him.

"He is such a good father! I'll talk to you later. Keep up the good work!" Adam said and laughed.

"The walking Mr. M … Aunt Eunice he did an amazing job!" Janice held her mouth and laughed into her hand as she quickly followed Adam.

"I am proud of you!" Eunice told Marcus.

"I like that girl. She and Adam must come up and see us more often, and bring that adorable child of theirs. He was laughing and having himself a good time with me!" Marcus said.

Guy and Tate were back at GM & GS Private Investigation Service reviewing a few cases that were still open. Guy began answering requests to hire them for their investigating expertise.

Mrs. Cothran was clearly emotional trying to get the evidence that she needed to prove her husband was having an affair. "I want to nail him to the wall. You guys have to help me and I will pay you good with my settlement monies."

Guy informed her, "We would be glad to look into this matter for you Mrs. Cothran, but we have to have one half of the fee up front to retain us. Then the other half on the completion of collecting the evidence, you requested."

"Okay I will get you the money by tomorrow at lunch time, and give you the names and my suspicions. I don't want anything on my computer … or phone that could come back to haunt me. I will give you my friend's phone number which will be my contact number and use her name," said Mrs. Cothran.

"And whom may I ask is your girlfriend?" he asked. Guy was writing everything down and got the name and number.

"Kathy Harper, the wife of the pastor at the Baptist Church down the road. 600-987-5432. Her first husband did the same thing to her. So she has been advising me," she told him.

"I see. Well the best advise is to go about as usual, and be careful. Don't say anything to any female that may tell her husband, because their hubby will call your hubby. It's a proven fact," Guy stated.

"See you tomorrow," he hung up. He and Tate planned their method of gathering information, but would not start until the money was in their hands.

CHAPTER THREE

The triplets were eleven now and playing volleyball. It was a coed team in the summer and all three were die hard volleyball enthusiasts. Jill, Jessie, and Johnny were on the same team and they were fierce.

"Nothing gets passed them," the parents screamed.

Beatrice and Roscoe were doting parents and hearing praise from other parents was music to their ears. Of course, the opponents had a few choice words, also.

Roscoe treated all seven of them to milkshakes because of their win. Beatrice was beaming and holding Roscoe's hand.

"Dad you're the best," echoed seven times.

"Alright already! When you guys win, we get milkshakes every time. Deal?" he high-five them all.

"When finished, head for the WAGON TRAIN!" That was their nickname for the Mercedes-Benz Sprinter van. It seated nine easily with equipment for games. It was a workhorse.

Their first rule was "No Food or Drink in the van."

So far they all had complied, but Roscoe. Beatrice had caught him eating a cheeseburger in the van. She reprimanded him in private.

"My poor baby was hungry! Don't let me have to spank you twice in one week," and she winked.

The kids were racing for the van. Roscoe was limping where his foot had gone to sleep, he told the kids.

Beatrice had done it again. He had to lean forward and pretend pain, and she laughed with her little short top on and gingham shorts that rose when she sat. "Wowie! Long legs!"

Madeline and Trevor went with Jasmine & John to sign with the contractor to build the house. They had approved the blueprints. The contractor asked, "Why did you sign Robert when your name is John?"

"That's my stage name. I'm an actor," and grinned at his wife. Trevor nodded to the contractor as if to say it's legit.

The house was on a time schedule like the others around the clock … massive teamwork and security for this house.

"This is a day that I have always dreamed about!" Jasmine was crying again. She never cried.

Madeline asked, "Are you pregnant dear? That's what I did for the first three months. Jasmine looked at John and he paled. Then he picked her up and said, "I sure hope so!"

"We got to go to the drugstore folks, and we'll meet you back at the house," John was still carrying Jasmine like a baby to the car.

"Madeline if she isn't, that boy is going to be so unhappy!" Trevor said what he had observed.

"I know me and my big mouth. Trev I know I am right!" GM stated as fact.

"We will see. We will see, Mama Hen!" and he kissed her.

Jasmine got the pregnancy test kit. She had never thought about it because she had never been regular. That wasn't new, if she missed a month before. She just said, "Hallelujah!"

He didn't trust her. He held the stick, "I have never heard of a man doing this!" she said. He said, "I'm not normal."

"You are though! You my dear Lass, you are pregnant with my baby!" He picked her up as if she was a porcelain doll and sat her down on their bed. They both cried with joy!

"Happy tears! I love you so much. This is a blessing from above. The house will be built and decorated before him or her gets here," John said.

"Let's go tell the others. Madeline first!" Jasmine said.

"The lady deserves a medal for that piece of information. She can suggest a doctor for you. I want you to have the best!" John commanded.

"Speaking of babies, where is Clancy?" she asked.

Trevor frowned, "In my chair. He took it away from me the first night. Haven't been able to get it back since!"

He laughed and so did everyone else and Clancy howled.

"Your dogs seem to get along with him and I am so glad. Come here boy!" Clancy ambled over to John and licked Jasmine's face.

"Guess what Madeline?" Jasmine quipped.

"What, dear?" and GM inhaled deeply.

"I am pregnant! So the bathroom stick says. You were right!" Jasmine hugged her as Madeline was shaking her head at Trevor in the affirmative 'I told you so' manner.

"Do you know of a good doctor?" Jasmine asked with John hanging over her back to hear.

"Dr. Silverstein is the best!" Adriana came through the door with Unitus toting the two kids.

"He let's you have sex in his office and charges the insurance company for that thirty minutes. Oops! I wasn't suppose to say that was I. Dearest, Darling, the love of my life. Sorry!" she grinned and cooed at Unitus.

"Any other secrets YOU would like to share with the world? No, don't dare open your mouth again. I can't have you tell them all, tonight. Let's wait until tomorrow!" Unitus was laughing so hard the children were swinging like monkeys from his arms.

"Yes, John! Dr. Silverstein is the best!" Unitus said winking.

"My kind of doctor!" John was grinning and rubbing Jasmine's tummy that was not in anyways a bump, but a flat abs stomach.

"Should I worry! No stop John, you are being ridiculous!" he said to himself.

The more he rubbed, the more she backed up against him. Both were feeling it arising to a situation that was calling for drastic measures.

"No darling … yes you are going to have to lay down for a few minutes and REST," and she nodded to him.

"I agree that is a good idea," she answered and bit her lip. He maneuvered her through the crowd to their room where they could celebrate the unofficial news.

Her tummy was so small. How can it be? He kissed her belly and she buried his head in her breasts. He was ready and eased into paradise!

She gasped,"O my word! This is what makes me stop crying," and she moaned.

Around and around she went, and he was holding on by one thin thread, knowing she had to finish before him. Then she would do it for him better and no one or nothing could ever break this bond ... a marriage of body and soul.

The summer was ending and Bruce was preparing all his staff for the return of the students. Their curriculum was actually the best he had ever seen. He had hired some special education teachers that the law required because last year's staff had quit.

The school had some parents that liked to dictate what their kids would and would not do. He was able to deal with them and offer "suggestions" and let them pick the one of the authorized options.

They did not even realize it was the one, he wanted them to chose from the beginning. By putting two off the wall ones with that one, he knew they would choose the best one ... HIS choice.

The teachers were adequate and he was going to work on getting them excited about an incentive pay for the best teacher of the year. They would all want to be the best.

He was going to sit in the classrooms, and see how the kids were focusing. If not at all, then he'd make suggestions to capture their minds, and make them want to learn. Make it interesting, his grade teachers sure did. But they were the best money could buy, and he had to bring that to these kids. Not with money, leading by example was his new motto.

He was exhausted when he got home. He talked so much. Jana went and got a thermometer to take his temperature.

That brought him back to reality!

She smiled at him and said, "Relax."

"Honey I'm home!" He would always announce like Ricky Ricardo. "Lucy, where are you?"

He remembered, what they did next when they found each other and smiled!

Kyleigh was home alone with Madison in school, and Guy back to work. She called Beatrice who was the same. She still had a housekeeper that helped with the mass of washing and ironing the clothes for the kids, and some cooking. Beatrice's day was mostly alone time with Roscoe at work.

When Kyleigh called, it was happiness to plan a day out.

"I'll pick you up in ten minutes," Kyleigh hung up.

"We are going rollerblading," Kyleigh said.

"You are crazy, if you think I am going to damage this pearly white legs that Roscoe loves so well!" Beatrice stated.

"Oh shut up, Spoil Sport! I was kidding. I'd probably bust my asre and couldn't give Guy what he wants every day!" she grinned while Face Timing on her phone at her best friend.

No subject was off limits, "I want to get a Brazilian wax!" Kyleigh said adamantly.

"You can't be serious. You want to pay someone one to rip your crotch out, and not have sex for a week because it hurts so bad," Beatrice frowned and made a distorted face.

"Oh No! You have already done it and did not tell me!"

"I was so ashamed and I told you I hurt from menstrual cramps. What a lie! Sorry forgive, but don't do it honey!"

"Okay. I want a tattoo of a teeny tiny daisy on the back of my neck," Kyleigh said.

"Sounds good. I know the place. One of the neurosurgeon's medical student that I know works at this exclusive TAT parlor. He can put a ring through your labia. Oops!"

She crossed her legs as if in pain.

"You are kidding. Did YOU?" Kyleigh gasped.

"No. Do I look like an idiot?" Beatrice asked and frowned.

"Well? Don't answer that! On any given day I sway back and forth," then Beatrice giggled.

"You keep me sane. Only you my friend knows, how crazy I am!" and Kyleigh was thankful to have Beatrice as a true friend.

"Takes one to know one," Beatrice said nonchalantly as she finished filing her last fingernail, and looked up with a wide grin.

"The point is he and she are good. The daisy will be a sterile technique, truly safe. Yeah!" Beatrice quoted.

"Yeah!" Kyleigh said as if a light bulb had gone off in her head.

"Back up! You don't have a ring in your whooha, do you Beatrice? B fess up!"

"No, I have my nipples pierced," and killed herself laughing at the look on Kyleigh's face.

Beatrice said, "No way … nada. I am chicken... cluck cluck cluck! If you get the teeny tiny daisy on your neck, I will get the teeny tiny four leaf clover on a buttock. Okay?"

K said, "Yeah, but we must do it at the same time though."

They sat in chairs side by side at the TAT parlor. Kyleigh said, "Guy is going to kill me!"

"I know and Roscoe is going to kill me! But it is exciting OWIE … OWIE!" she said softly.

"Ouch! Ouch! Ouch! Oh my goodness it hurts," Kyleigh said screaming at the tattooist.

She said, "Are you sure you have had a baby? This should be a piece of cake. Almost through, honey!" Kyleigh fainted.

Beatrice said, "They gave her drugs with her C-section. She didn't feel a thing. She'll be fine! Let me see. Oh Kyleigh, it is so cuteeeeeee!" she winked at the TAT girl.

Kyleigh snapped up and grabbed the hand mirror, "Let me see! Let me see! Aww… It is perfect. Thank you!" and hugged her TAT girl.

"Hey, big Red! Why didn't you howl like she did?" her TAT girl asked.

Beatrice said, "I've had seven children and all natural. I was funning with the two owies to make K over here feel better. It was a piece of cake."

The TAT girl said, "SEVEN?" and the TAT girl fainted.

"We can't show them for a week," Beatrice said.

"I will do my best to keep the collar up in the back, but my nightie is going to be the down fall!" Kyleigh said.

"Well cut the lights off silly! Or take charge, get on top! He can't see the back of your neck that way!" Beatrice suggested.

"That is a very good idea. Take Charge! Take the bull by the horns!" Kyleigh was all over the road.

"Okay K … take it easy. You HAVE been on top before?"

Beatrice had to ask.

"I did on our honeymoon before …before." She began crying so hard Beatrice had to steer off the road from the passenger side of the vehicle. "Step on the brake, Hon!"

They parked the car and walked up and down the sidewalk as Kyleigh relived some moments that she had not shared even with Guy. He, she knew could not handle it. Beatrice was about to cave herself, but no she had to be strong and listen as Kyleigh spilled her guts. HOW she was mutilated by Jared Banks!

"This being in prison at Madeline and Trevor's was a reminder that no one is safe from monsters like them. I hate them! I hate! When will it end?" Kyleigh hugged her friend.

"Make it stop!" Kyleigh begged. This was a bad flashback.

"Honey, I wish I could. You just talk to me anytime. Get it out! I am here for you. Show that pretty daisy to Guy tonight and he will try and eat it off of you! Nothing else matters!" and she smiled at Kyleigh until she smiled back.

"This has been the best day ever! I needed to talk!" Kyleigh said and dried her tears.

"Want to see my 4 leaf clover?" Beatrice asked.

"B put your dress down!" K said and was laughing again.

CHAPTER FOUR

Corey was in his last semester of college. He had decided to major in auto mechanics and he had excelled in foreign car repairs. He was going to open a business like Adam had. He had to get his degree to manage the financial part of the business. Marcus had insisted.

Marcus was going to help him get started. He was amazing with all his troubles, he never forgot about Corey and Ellen. He included them in everything.

Unitus had asked Marcus, if he wanted to prosecute the FBI especially Sterling. He declined.

"If they clear my name and keep that Jung fellow behind bars or give him the death sentence," Marcus grinned

"I will not, but if he ever gets OUT. I will go after Sterling's throat," Marcus promised and he paused.

"I have no hate for the FBI. I have seen them in action the time before this. They are a great group of guys," he added.

Unitus went and saw Sterling and told him what Marcus had said.

Sterling said, "I can't believe, he didn't go after my jugular.

I know I WOULD HAVE! Unitus, the judge said he would meet with us today."

"Can Marcus come at three this afternoon?" he asked.

"I will have him here!" Unitus shook his hand.

Marcus, Adriana, and Unitus sat on the front row.

Sterling said, "The FBI made a grave mistake in accusing Mr. Buchanan and we want his name cleared."

"Mr. Buchanan, do you intend to sue?" the judge asked.

Unitus stood, "No Your Honor, but he would like the FBI to place a notice in every major newspaper across the USA that states he was falsely accused. They have agreed. So let it be noted. This should clear his name and restore his good reputation."

The judge sat and looked at Sterling and his agents, "You are very lucky this fine man did not sue. Do what you promised, and this case is dismissed. Both parties sign the papers, and I will sign them in my chambers. Unitus will you be returning to the DA's office on Monday?"

"Yes, Your Honor. I will be here," Unitus replied.

"All rise …" the bailiff announced.

The judge struck the gavel on the desk and said, "This court is adjourned," and he left by the back door to his chambers.

Adriana and Unitus both hugged Marcus, and he was all smiles. They would pick up Eunice and take them to THE INN which was Marcus's and her favorite restaurant.

Eunice was so proud of him, and she was glad Marcus had recovered so much. He was walking more and eating wiser. She was pampering him and he was loving it.

"It takes time, dear!" she cuddled with him in front of them.

"Adriana have I told you lately what a fine choice you made in picking your own husband, and having the good sense to reject the ones I sent your way?" Marcus asked.

"No Daddy you haven't. Yes, he is a fine specimen of a man and I am so proud of his ...." Adriana was cut off.

"Honey that is enough! Thank you both!" Unitus said and her eyes widened. They had barely spoken until they got home.

Adriana's eyes were shooting daggers, "What do you mean by cutting me off? I have things I wanted to say!"

"Honey! Let's put the kids to bed and we will talk all you want. Okay Sweetums?" Unitus was putting Vanderbilt to bed and he was almost asleep.

He went in as Adriana was kissing Angel goodnight, and he kissed her. She snuggled under the covers. They tiptoed out.

"You scare me, Adriana! After what you said about the doctor. Lord knows what you were going to tell your father," he was waiting.

"I was going to say how much I admire my husband and the way he handled himself against the dreaded FBI which my father should have sued. He said you asked him, and he declined." She was prancing and unbuttoning her dress of pale blue to match her eyes. Her high heels came off.

"I would never tell my daddy, how I lust after my husband," Unitus was swallowing hard the lump in his throat, "and I pant after his..." and she touched him, walked around and put her hands on his massive back.

Rubbed it vigorously at all his overly sensitive places, grabbed his buttocks, then put her hands in his pockets as she kissed down his spine.

She had stepped out of her dress, but he had not noticed. He was under her spell of seduction. She came around in front of him and he saw she had no clothes on.

He lifted her over his shoulders.

"Do that Tarzan yell" she whispered in his ear. "Wake me up, not the kids!"

"Open … That's it!" he said.

"Yell into my mouth how good it feels," mumble … mumble …

The doctor visit was a mere formality and it confirmed the pregnancy. John was smiling like he had swallowed a canary.

Jasmine was numb, "Really! This is not a dream?"

"No, this is for real, love!" John said.

"Are you sure you can handle me … and a baby … and a dog … and a house … and a family?" Jasmine paused.

"I am counting my blessings. My love that grows for you is only increasing. I forgot to ask him, why I am crying so much?" Jasmine chided her.

He laughed, "I know what can stop it and you do, too!"

"OMG we are going to have to get out of here! I feel like I am going to cry from happiness," Jasmine said.

"Let's go and tell the others. Officially we are going to be parents, and I have to go by the bank," John stated.

He went in and she sat in the car. She knocked on James's connecting window and said "We are going to have a baby. You are the first to officially know!"

"I am honored. Congrats to you and Robert, I mean John," James said. She saw her two bodyguards from her compact mirror while she was touching up her tear tracks.

John slid in, "You look beautiful with or without makeup."

"John.... we....are....going....to....have... a baby!" she said breathless.

"I know and now rest the little one, and let me just hold you." John and she fell asleep in the limo. They had been so anxious last night that they couldn't sleep.

James could not bring himself to wake them and ask Mrs. Madeline to do it.

"Okay kids rise and shine," they both stretched and Clancy came barking. They went inside the house with the news.

Tate and Guy had begun the investigation as soon as the money was in their banking account. Tate followed Mr. Cothran on his motorbike, and stopped as the man went into the local market. Cothran stood talking to a female.

Tate took pictures with his phone.

"Probably nothing," Tate told himself. Then he went to a nearby ice cream parlor and came outside to to talk to another woman and Tate got that picture also.

"This man is definitely a ladies man," Tate said to himself as he followed him to two more places of businesses and then he stopped by a house. Tate wrote down the address. He stayed two hours, and Tate was eating a candy bar.

The woman was waving goodbye and he blew her a kiss! "Bingo! Maybe his sister? Yeah right!" and laughed. Then Luke went to his own house for two hours.

Then he went to his work office.

Tate phoned Guy. "It is your turn to watch his dude. I got to eat. I got a lot of pictures on my phone. Hurry and get here. My stomach is growling." He put his phone to his belly and hung up, and began laughing.

Guy came around the corner and they talked awhile watching Luke Cothran's door.

"Tate that is one bad tiger you got in your tank. Debbie must have a heck of a time feeding him," Guy grinned.

Tate left and got a burger and called Debbie, "Just wanted to hear your sweet voice."

"Jasmine is pregnant!" she hung up so she could cry.

Everyone was having babies, but them. She didn't realize how bad it would hurt to watch everyone having their own baby, and her not to be able to give Tate one. He must be disappointed, too.

One hour later, Tate was walking into their bedroom. He told Guy he had to leave early that Debbie needed him.

She had fallen asleep and there was a box of Kleenex on the bed beside her, and she had one in her hand. He sat on their sofa watching her breathe, and thinking of the right words.

She awoke slowly and saw him. She bounced off the bed and put the box behind her, and smiled.

"Debbie we have to talk. Come sit with me," Tate was hoping he could say how he felt, and ease her mind.

Tate held her and looked into her eyes. The gang rape had destroyed her female reproductive organs. She had to have the operation, a hysterectomy. It was necessary. It was a fact.

"Honey I know you want a baby or do you? If you are thinking, I am sad without a child, YOU are wrong. I want you and only you. We have a lot of babies in our lives that we can play with, and thank goodness give them back after we get tired of them," he pointed out. Then he continued.

"I don't want any children, if I can't have you. I love you! Just like you are! Just like I knew you were ... when I married you. You are my all! Don't ever cry about that ever!" and he kissed her and held her. She hadn't spoken.

"If you ever want to adopt, we will, but not anytime soon please. I am not ready" and he laughed. "I am too immature. I love that word. Means I am still young. Any questions?"

She was smiling, "No."

Guy was walking down the street browsing. Luke got in his car and Guy had to scramble, but he caught up with him at a distance, and the man had gone home.

He would come back in a couple of hours, and see if he was home. He was going to have to place a bug under the fender to track him. He could have his wife to place it ... even better.

He would run by the office and get it, and she did not want to be called at home, so he called her BFF, Kathy's number.

He could meet her at this girlfriend's house. Agnes D. Cothran was there at the time that he specified.

"Yes he is at home showering, and I will be glad to place it. Just show me how," and she learned.

She dropped her earring on the ground by her husband's car and reached under, and placed the tracking device. Luke came and asked, "What are you doing Agnes?" he was frowning.

She picked the earring up and showed it to him. "I found it! I found it! I saw my diamond earring when it hit my blouse and dropped. These are the expensive ones you got me on our honeymoon!" and she placed it back in her ear and smiled.

"I am truly glad you found that one. It cost me an arm and a leg," and he laughed.

"I have a meeting and it maybe late when I get back, so don't wait up, Honey!" he said as he got in his Thunderbird classic car.

She smiled and waved, blowing him a kiss.

"You dirty, good for nothing, rotten catfish, slimy WORM for a husband! I am going to catch you. So have yourself a good old time, dear!" and she walked back into the house.

She put her earrings in her new safe, not his safe because they were worth a small fortune.

Guy got a whiff of Kyleigh's favorite perfume. Oh my goodness! There she stood in a red teddy with her hair pulled up and dang red high heels, too! He walked back out the door and closed it, and he walked back in to her. She was giggling.

"Yes, I do believe this is my house! Could it be our anniversary? No. It's not my birthday! Where is MADISON?" his eyes popped out in a panic because he was fully aroused.

"Calm down darling. He is spending the night with Cain and Caleb. It is a special night," and she walked closer. A night you won't forget, and it maybe a night you pop your cork!" she said licking her lips.

"You can take that to the bank and count on it!" Guy said as he walked toward her.

She said, "You may not like what I did today. It was very … very … naughty."

He swallowed hard, "Oh my dear! What did you do? No don't tell me. I don't want to know because you have gone out of your way to drive me up and down this wall from needing you. Don't make me wait any longer!"

She walked toward him, "I might as well confess," and she turned and he grabbed her. As he was going to kiss her neck, she extended it to one side.

He saw it. "You got a tattoo … it is beautiful," and he kissed it and kissed it. His hands were everywhere.

"You are not mad?" she asked.

Questioning why? She waited.

"No, if you like it, I love it and I intend to get one, too!" he kissed her passionately.

"Of what might I ask ?" she looked at him sideways and wrapped one leg around him.

"The word NAUGHTY! Now where would you like it to be?" he asked. She whispered the place.

"So be it!" he said and continued to walk up the steps with her in his arms.

"I am going to be naughty naughty naughty all night!" he said smiling.

"You had better be because we have to return the favor," she laughed on every step.

He dropped her on the bed, "You have got to be kidding!"

"All seven?" Guy asked and held his head with both hands. She had informed him they had to babysit Roscoe's seven children in return for tonight.

"But if you don't think I am worth it. I can go get Madison," and she began putting her heels back on, and pouting.

Guy took her shoes away and flung them to the floor, and climbed between her legs.

"You are totally worth it! Bring on another seven, and I'd say the same." he thoroughly kissed her and Kyleigh was gasping for air.

He grinned, "You are playing hard to get?"

She said, "Roll over mister. I'm in charge tonight! Now take those pants off."

He was popping the buttons and wrecking the zipper on his good pants, "Yes ma'am!"

"Now lay down and let me have my way with you," she had her soft hands on him and he was looking at the ceiling.

"Holy crap you got to hurry up, before you have nothing to work with!" and she did it.

All for a tattoo. Right?

CHAPTER FIVE

The mountain vista from Trevor's was being occupied by bulldozers and logging trucks. On one of those trucks was Kirk Matterson. He had no idea whose place this was, but it was a good paying lumberjack job.

He was lucky to get the job. The man driving the truck was Bryce, a friend from his school days that had done good for himself.

"If you keep your nose clean, ya 'll do fine. I ain't havin' no druggie workin' fer me! Ya hear?" Bryce made it clear.

"I promise those days are long gone. Don't you worry I am clean! Nothing would make me do that again," and frowned as he looked out the truck window.

They had stopped for gas and there she was on the back of that motorbike and he felt a "twinge." He told himself look away, but he couldn't. A man got on the bike and they rode off toward the work site.

"What's wrong with you? Ya look like ya seen a dag-gum ghost!" Bryce asked.

"Nothing just thought I saw someone I knew. No, it couldn't have been!" and Kirk shook his head.

"Just seeing things," and he laughed.

"It must've been a dag-burn good daydream!" and he laughed and pulled out into traffic.

"Oh she was mighty fine! Pretty as a picture and felt like butter in my hands!" Kirk was smiling at the mountains.

"Ya shut ya mouth for ya have ME dreamin', gotta drive!" Bryce said and rounded the curve.

Kirk was still thinking about that gorgeous woman chef.

Bruce was becoming a valuable asset to the private school. The kids and the parents were all singing his praises. Jana was so proud of him, and he felt useful for the first time in a long long while.

Jana in her navy blue suit with that three inch slit up the back was swaying down the hallway toward the door, and her heels were clicking to his heartbeat.

Boy, did he love that little woman ... all five foot two inches of her. Tonight was their community service night and afterward she would be served all she could eat.

When they arrived home Trevor and Madeline said, "You two look so handsome the school atmosphere really agrees with both of you!"

They had stopped for some loving on the way home. The spa was on the way home from the food shelter where they had bagged food for the homeless.

The spa treatment was a nice massage together. Looking at each other and asking if he could have some alone time with his wife, turned out to be more when they got in the car.

"We aren't going to make it home. What do you want us to do?" She was kissing his neck and straddling him in the car.

"This parking lot is not well lit. Just take it. I have no undies," and he did. From a distance, all you could see was one person.

They were being discreet. No wailing just easy steady sex that peaked with nothing, but need and wonderful release. "Yes!"

"This is just an appetizer for you till I can get you home," he said and pulled harder till she squealed, "Bruce! Bruce!"

Madeline was so happy all her brood was home. She and Trevor rode the trike up to the work site and walked around. He wanted her to see it up close and the foundation was already poured.

The framing had been started on one side, and the progress was amazing. The three shifts were working diligently to finish on time.

Lefty came to speak to his favorite woman in the world. If it hadn't been for Madeline, he would not have this foreman job at this construction company. The monster Chris Shackleford that cut his arm off, was dead. When he was caught, Lefty's anger died. His death was just icing on the cake.

"Hey Miss Madeline! How are you two doing?" Lefty said and shook Trevor's hand with his good hand.

"I am doing great now that I know you are overseeing my Jasmine's house," GM said.

"I will make sure it is done right. You two can count on me. Tell Roscoe I said hi, and to drop by and see me when he can. I got to get back to work, or the men will miss me barking at them," and Lefty laughed and went back down the hill.

GM waved as did Trevor. They got back on the trike and rode awhile because he knew she loved to ride in the fall.

He kept on going until they got to GM & GS Private Investigation Service's office.

Guy and Tate were busy at work on three cases.

GM strolled in asking, "Do you boys need any help?"

"Boy... do we ever," GS said.

Then he looked at Trevor, "Nope, we 're good!"

Luke Cothran had gone way away from town almost to Charlotte, and he did not go to a motel. He went to the Ballantyeme, a five star classy hotel. He met up with Francine a beautiful French woman, and he kissed her mercilessly.

Tate had followed and took pictures, and asked the desk if he had any idea when the next golf tournament was going to be held here. He got a brochure as he watched what floor the two lovebirds went on, and the winning number was five.

He also ask, "How much for a room here?" he laughed.

"Just kidding got to go meet the family," and went to the fifth floor. They were still kissing in front of Room 5200. He took a picture and flew back to the elevator, and out the front door, and got on his bike speeding home.

He phoned Guy. "Got it! Can't wait for you to see and Miss Agnes is going to flip when she see this one! You even won't believe this one!"

The next morning he went by Walmart and developed all the pictures with the dates and time stamped by his camera phone. He made two copies that was a must. He put them in an envelope, and handed them to Guy.

"Dang you are good, partner. How in the world did you get these?" he asked.

"Investigation is my specialty. I've been snooping all my life. Had to when small and people would pay me to keep my mouth shut," said Tate and smiled.

"This guy though may kill us, if his wife cleans him out," Guy reminded Tate.

"You are right and the device is still under his car. So do we need anything else?" Tate asked.

"No this is more than enough!" Guy declared.

Agnes looked at the pictures at Kathy's house with Guy present and nearly fainted.

"I will hire my attorney until then ... you put these in your strongest safe, and guard them with your life," she pleaded.

"He will not have a leg to stand on. He has some unsavory characters that work for him. BE CAREFUL. My lawyers, Maple & Hook can and will fight for me. After I retain them. I will give them the pictures then. I have to do it this week after he goes to one of his weekly meetings that takes all day," Agnes was thinking out loud.

"Thank you for everything I will write you a check for the remaining monies. I have my own bank account. This was my father's business when we married. I put enough monies in this private account in case something like this happened."

Kathy hugged her and let her cry.

"I will be going. Call me Kathy, if she needs us," and Guy left. He did not feel good about this at all.

He needed to talk to Roscoe and have him get information on any unsavory characters this man had working for him.

They could have Trevor run it through his database as well.

Kyleigh is going to freak! If they have to go back to hiding again, but better be safe than sorry.

Tate had to know this, too. His picture would be on the security cameras at the hotel. Holy crap! This business is not what Guy was hoping for a simple diversion from the day to day routine. That was all it should have been. He had no idea how rich these folks were. He was well off himself, but poor growing up. He loved detective work when he was single.

The next day Tate and he went over to Trevor's.

"Now what have you 'all got into … Roscoe you don't look so good. Guy you look worse. Tate you have no idea the severity of what you are into, do you?" Trevor had sized it even before they told him. Then they told him everything.

"I thought you'd be proud," Tate hung his head.

"Don't leave the house. You are grounded," Trevor said.

"I say it because I love you and this man will be after you make no bones about it. If the wife is after his money. He will want those pictures at any cost," Trevor had to lay it out for him.

"Where are those pictures Guy?" Trevor asked.

"In the bank in my safe deposit box!" Guy said.

"Good that was smart! I love you, too. So you are grounded, too. Bring Kyleigh and Madison here for the time being. It is better to be safe than sorry. Okay son?" Trevor looked him in the eyes. Same thing he had thought earlier.

Roscoe said, "Trevor they are new at this detective work."

Guy bucked him, "I graduated the top of my class and I thought it was a simple divorce case. How was I to know he is a scum maggot! I should have researched the family history more thoroughly than I did. I admit that Roscoe."

"Yes hindsight is a teacher!" MADELINE said.

She had heard it all.

"Tate has no idea about what this family has gone through. But you three have time to tell him while you are sitting here looking at each other. Tate you did a good job! It is that your life maybe in jeopardy with the camera's videoing you as you snapped those pictures," and she hugged him.

Jasmine and John came into a somber group of people. She looked at John, "Something is wrong. Madeline what is it?"

"Your brothers will have plenty of time to tell you. You all are grounded till further notice and you boys go get your families and bring them home," GM said.

Tate didn't know how to tell Debbie, but he did.

"Okay mister we are joined at the hip," Debbie said.

Jana said, "Bruce has to work. The school is counting on him. We could stay near it for the time being. I will call him and ask him what he wants to do?"

Guy said, "The woman has not confronted him so we will have time to make plans until he sees the pictures. I just don't know what she will tell him in her anger. We just need to be ready. The security is in place and bodyguards for all. So just go about your usual routines for today. Is that okay Trevor? Little brother is who we are protecting this time."

Roscoe said, "And you GS!" and he hugged Guy.

"Get off me, Bro! You can't whip my butt anymore!" and they started shadow boxing. It had always been their way of unwinding since they were little.

"Okay boys that's enough LOVE. Go ! Get! Do what you gotta do!" GM said and she hugged Trevor.

Bruce had opted to stay at a Best Western for the duration.

They had an efficiency suite and he rented it for a month starting tomorrow night. "That will give us time to pack and get out of the firing line. I hate it but Trevor and the boys will keep everyone safe. Jana you are my wife, you and I know we are not in on this one. I agree this is best and it will free a room up for the others. I will talk to mother when I get home. I love you!" Bruce said and hung up.

Jasmine and John could not believe this, but she was crying all the time anyway. The hormones were raging. She smiled at John, "I'm okay but you have never been in a family like mine."

"It is good to have a family" and he rubbed her tummy. He added, "I might as well get use to it because we are living next door darling!" and he kissed her tears away.

She was rubbing Clancy's head and smiling, "This is true!" He had a way of making her feel safe in the midst of chaos. All she had to do was look into his eyes and everything else faded away.

Tate took Debbie to their room. Debbie just wanted them to be alone and let Tate talk about it. He did and told her about the cheating husband and the pictures. How he did his job too well!

She said, "This family will take care of us and we can enjoy this time together. She was so scared for him, but did not want to show it. "Tate just don't leave me!" she said.

Roscoe told Beatrice and she started crying, "Kyleigh just said yesterday that she couldn't take it again, if they had to hide out. Roscoe you have no idea what happened to her when she was kidnapped. She told me things that broke my heart. Each time she has worse flashbacks. If she finds out that Guy is in jeopardy, she may revert back to the way she was in Dallas."

"OH MY! Everything will be alright my crew will protect us, all of us. I have good people in my company. You and K will be doing your own thing. So make some plans of what you think will keep her cheerful. I know this is killing Guy because his business has caused this mayhem. Trevor didn't look good. He is the one I am worried about. I thought he was going to strangle Guy for putting Tate in this danger," he paused and rubbed his head.

"There I go again defending little brother. He screwed up. I have done stupid things, too. He has always helped me through them. I will be there for him now, too. That's what families do they stick together."

Beatrice let him talk it out and had not said a word. Roscoe looked back, and she was fast asleep. "That is the only time she is quiet!" he chuckled. It was good to talk it out even if it was to himself. He stretched out and tried to go to sleep.

He would get his family over to GM 's tomorrow afternoon.

He didn't see any rush unless this Cothran woman says something stupid to her husband. Now he was wide awake.

CHAPTER SIX

Tate had called Adam, his big brother. "I did a good job. It just back fired. The thing is stay away until this is all over. Tell the rest. I don't want anyone getting hurt on my account. Ask Aunt Eunice to tell Adriana and Unitus and explain the situation that it is a secret until the Cothran woman tells her husband about the pictures. Trevor may tell Unitus and Marcus, but I wanted to explain to you guys myself. Kiss my nephew for me. Night!"

Adam said, "Goodnight bro!" he had let him talk it out.

He told Janice and kissed Andy for Tate.

Janice said, "What a difference a week makes. He has been working for Guy what a week maybe two and he used all his skills he learned at school, but they forgot to teach him street smarts. When I was in the police academy, they didn't teach me that either," she shook her head remembering.

"I did some stupid things when I was assigned a beat. It took time to live those mistakes down. Tate will be fine. It will just take some time. You have to make some mistakes to grow and learn from them," she consoled Adam.

"He needs to hear that. How about you tell him just that. He knows you were a police officer before becoming a security guard. I am so glad I met you when I did. It would have freaked me out to think you were on the street at night. Fighting the bad guys like me," he stared into her eyes with panic.

"Oh I would have arrested you for carrying a concealed weapon," and Janice grabbed him.

"You need a permit for that!" and made him laugh and he grabbed her for a kiss and then more kisses.

Trevor had got the information and it was not good. "It seems Mr. Cothran took over for Agnes's father, and has run the shipping company since the old man died. He is into shipping large crates of weapons. Yes, guns or whatever. His business is filling military arsenals. He was suspected of drug smuggling, but it has never been proven," he paced the den.

"This Frenchwoman is a dealer in ammunition in France and he is being set up for the kill. She wants to emerge her company with his. Pun intended. He is fascinated by her and would leave the Mrs. in a heartbeat, if not for one thing. She owns one half of the stocks, and he cannot buy or sell without her signature," he looked at the boys.

"This is going to be a vicious divorce and truly someone could get killed. Guy has the key to his madness, and Tate is a potential witness to his infidelity as well as the photo taker."

John and Jasmine were also invited to the meeting.

"Madeline what do you suggest," he wanted her included because she had the most to lose.

"Call in the big dogs and let us all start a storyboard like none other," and she got busy organizing.

Kyleigh and Guy started doing their thing as they did from the conception of GM & GS Private Investigation Service when teenagers.

Beatrice was amazed at how Kyleigh was working on it. This was giving her something to focus on, and help her husband.

Jasmine admitted she was an ace at weaponry. "I can ID every piece. Take it a part and put it back manually with speed. The problem is, if he is dealing in smuggling. I will know them. If I identify them, they will have a greater need to kill me," Jasmine paled.

John just stood there taking it all in. Then he said, "There is something I forgot to tell you 'all. I am not just Jasmine's hubby. I am the designer of aeronautic weaponry. I designed the Softpoint located on the airframes of a plane. So I know about the aircraft gun pods, things the average person would not know about that being the INTERNAL and EXTERNAL bombs and their mechanisms. If these characters are dealing in Aircraft weaponry, I am your man. I can dismantle it and assemble it with speed," looking at Jasmine.

Trevor knew this to be true, but he was going to let Robert now John divulge it in his own good time.

Jasmine looked at her husband. She was impressed. She was getting very warm all of a sudden. She rubbed her tummy and he saw it.

"We may have a little Einstein here," he kissed her hair and rubbed her tummy until she grabbed his hand to steady herself. She was shivering!

"Are you cold, love?" John was concerned.

She shook her head staring at him, "the opposite."

He smiled and announced, "We are going, Jasmine needs to lay down," and he escorted her to their room.

"I am on fire. You have set me on fire. Dismantle me!"

"I will gladly, if you think you can put me back together manually with speed," he said softly.

"I can't wait any longer!" she said.

"You don't have to! I'm shivering, too!"

"Here it comes! John hold me!"

"I got you! Let it go! The best weaponry of all is love!"

The construction project remained in full swing and Jasmine & John would not waste a minute of one day dwelling on the past. They were only focused on the future.

It was two months before the divorce court event of the century was now on the books. Agnes had thrown Luke out of her family home.

On his way out, she had the butler throw all his designer clothes on the ground and set a match to them. He stood there staring at Agnes, gritting his teeth.

"You will not dress in the clothes that I bought for you to see your trollop. Do not show your face at the business or the police will remove you for trespassing, my dear!" Agnes informed him with a smile.

"Oh ... half of everything is mine, my DEAR wife," and Luke spun off in his Thunderbird with the tracking device still attached.

She and her lawyers had blocked his every move. "Now my lawyers have the pictures." She had made it clear to him that she had them. So he would not pursue GM & GS Private Investigation team any longer.

She told him, "They no longer work for me Luke. I have a much better TEAM," and Agnes laughed a hardy laugh with no smile this time.

She was a shrewd businesswoman before she met this Casanova and she would be again. She had anticipated his every move. She dropped the bomb on him.

Luke went to the office, his pass did not work. He went to the shipyard, and he was escorted off. He called his men, and they did not answer. He went to get a room at the hotel, his credit cards were all frozen.

He called her. "You speak only to my lawyers. Hope she was worth it!" then Agnes blocked his calls.

"Madeline I know you want to help, but the boys have to learn to stand on their own two feet. We will not always be around," Trevor said.

He was right. She had to back off, but she was going to have a little fun with this man of hers. "You might not be around but I am going to live forever. Get me a young boy toy like the rest of these old …"

She didn't get to finish and he had her in his arms, "If I didn't know you were joking with me. I'd …"

"You'd what? Have your way with me? Please do!" and he showed her what an old man could do!

"Oh Trevor!" batting those eyelashes at him. He knew he had been used, and he just hoped she would continue batting those lashes for years to come.

"Now I do have things to do, not as important as you but things to research for Guy," Trevor said as he pulled on his boots.

"Okay see you at suppertime, big boy!" Madeline stretched.

"Oh crap! It can wait!" and he was back in the bed with her.

"Knock! Knock! Is anyone home?" Eunice said.

They scrambled to dress. It was the first day that everyone had gone back to their homes.

They came out of their bedroom not as well groomed as usual and welcomed Marcus and Eunice.

"Hope we didn't barge in, but I was worried something was wrong. That has been the case recently. We do apologize," she was looking at Marcus thinking it happens to us all the time.

Marcus told Trevor that his men had an eye on the freight line of the Cothrans, "Anything unusual they will let me know."

At that same time his phone rang, and his man had the news first hand that Luke Cothran had SHOT himself. "It should be on TV pretty soon. Just wanted you to know before hand."

"Thanks for calling. I appreciate it!" Marcus hung up and he turned to Trevor. "Cothran committed suicide!"

"I'll call the boys!" he text them instead since the grand kids had showed him how over and over. He kinda liked it.

Guy and Tate were working at GM & GS Private Investigation Service and turned on the office TV. Tate asked, "Is it finally over?"

"We will see. I sure hope so!" and they sat there waiting for the reporters to get their act together.

Mrs. Cothran was being interviewed. She was crying crocodile tears for the camera.

"She's a happy woman under those fake tears, but she is also lucky she had us working for her," Tate was expanding his chest.

"You and I are lucky, too. We learned a valuable lesson. Research our research, over and over, and plan ahead better. If pictures are to be taken it will be by a man in a good good disguise," he winked at Tate.

"Don't I know it! Debbie still isn't right," Tate admitted. "She thinks we are joined at the hip. Her phrase Partner."

"Kyleigh is the same, on pins and needles every day until I walk through that door. She says Partner, too!" Guy shared.

"What do you say we treat them to bowling and a nice dinner from this agency. It can be an expense write-off?" Guy agreed.

"You set it up and we will be there," Tate was working on another stolen car mystery. The third from a parking lot in the last year.

"What do you think about this case," Tate asked.

"Decline it, we need no more criminals in our lives," Guy easily answered that one.

"I agree," Tate was shifting through a stack and tossed that one into the rejection file box that they both had on their desks.

"The house next door has really gone up fast. I can't believe it has been three months," Tate was talkative today and Guy was trying to concentrate. He needed to give him some space.

"Yeah, it has. I ran into Robert the other day I mean John.

He says less than a month, they will be in. Jasmine is going to throw a big family party! So the wives will want us to go shopping for gifts. Yep! Going to get dragged to every store in town!" Guy said leaning back in his chair and chuckled.

"Not me, Debbie is a good online shopaholic! Grateful I am for the internet," and Tate smiled.

"I like the porno," and Tate ducked as Guy threw a wadded paper ball at him which he retrieve to throw back later.

"You call this work?" Madeline said as she walked in.

"No, Ma'am this is a needed break. What brings you out?" GS asked, but he knew it was the TV report.

Jasmine was four months pregnant and with big tops not preggy tops. You could barely tell she was with child.

Madeline kept saying," You got to eat for two!" and smiled.

Debbie was fixing healthy snacks for her and she was regularly hiking with John, and staying busy. Kyleigh was helping her make a scrapbook of photos.

Her main delight was sketching the wildlife at the lake. She never went without him and the bodyguards. John would fish with Trevor's blessing, and she would paint or sketch.

Jasmine looked at John, "Next month I will have new scenery on the other side of OUR new house."

He said, "And I'll have a shop to tinker in … in OUR new house."

"Do you think we should shop for furniture now or later," John asked earnestly.

"No I think we should lie on a mattress of air in every room and feel the spirit of the room and discuss," she rubbed him.

He threw the fishing pole down and scooped her up and said, "That is a marvelous idea! I think I will go over and tell those men to hurry a little faster."

She giggled in his ear. She was still light as a feather. No one was around the boathouse but them. She whispered, "Do you know what I am thinking?"

"That it is cold out here, and we should go in and build a fire?" John knew that was not it.

"Close! There is a nice kitchen in there and we could cook up a meal real fast on this OPEN flame?" patting her tummy.

Beatrice was fussing over the twin girls' hair, they were going to a cheerleader's competition and it needed to be tight so when they did their tumbling and flips, it would not get in the way of their vision.

"It is a safety feature. I am saving your lives!" Beatrice said as she finished. They were thirteen now, going on twenty.

"Don't be so dramatic Mom!" FiFi said. The echo was BeBe's voice agreeing with her sister.

"Okay, done! Next time you can fix it yourselves," Beatrice walked off to sit with Roscoe, and smiled at them.

"You wouldn't dare!" FiFi mouthing to her.

She shook her head, "Yes, I will young lady!"

BeBe said, "See what you have done! Pissed Mom off big time, and she will be on both our cases for a week!"

"Yep, but then we are free to roam. She will move on to terrorize Cain and Caleb, then the triplets. We will have a whole month to do what we wanna!" FiFi said.

She looked back and saw her father standing over them listening.

"Are my two beautiful cheerleaders plotting to overthrow the queen off her throne? It won't work. If that happens, she will be after me, and I will turn both of you over my knee!" Roscoe stated as fact.

"That is child abuse, Dad!" FiFi said. Looking up at him sweetly, batting her eyelashes like her mother had taught her.

"NO! Child abuse is when I cut those unlimited credit cards in half with a pair of scissors. Be nice to your Mom, girls!"

Madison was fourteen and a genius. He had skipped two grades and by next year would be attending college. His mother had kept reading materials around since birth that aspired him to learn more and more. He didn't have the siblings to occupy his time and he had turned to books mostly science to read. Guy and he were always doing experiments in the basement.

Kyleigh was so proud of her son, but he was at that age of discovering girls. Because he was so handsome, she prayed he would finish his college before dating. Guy laughed at her.

"You have got to be kidding, Kyleigh?"

"No I was hoping, you would give him the TALK," she said.

Guy said, "I talk to him every night!" She rolled her eyes.

"Oh, THE TALK! I did that last year. He is cool and does know about the birds and the bees," Guy said.

"I know he knows about pollination, but does he know how babies are created, Honey? Don't you dare laugh at me. He has been protected all his life. He is soon fifteen. I worry about those girls of ill- repute!" Kyleigh was pacing.

"Honey, Honey! He has had classes in sex education. Relax you got to let go. He will be fine! It's when he goes off to college you can start worrying," Guy winked at Madison who was standing behind his mother silently laughing.

Kyleigh turned, "That does it!" and put her hands on her hips.

"I will drive you to college young man every day! It's just down the road Madison. That 'll teach you to laugh at your mother!" stomping to her room with her arms crossed and a scowl on her face.

To Be Continued

Printed in the United States
By Bookmasters